MY THIR

Also by Daniela Krien in English translation

Someday We'll Tell Each Other Everything (2013)
Love in Five Acts (2021)
The Fire (2023)

DANIELA KRIEN

MY THIRD LIFE

Translated from the German
by Jamie Bulloch

MACLEHOSE PRESS
QUERCUS · LONDON

First published in German as *Mein drittes Leben* by
Diogenes Verlag AG, Zürich, in 2024
First published in Great Britain in 2026 by MacLehose Press
an imprint of Quercus
Part of John Murray Group

1

Line from *The Ice Palace* by Tarjei Vesaas, translated by Elizabeth Rokken
Lines from *The Brothers Karamazov* by Fyodor Dostoevksy,
translated by Constance Garnett

A CIP catalogue record for this book is available from the British Library

TPB ISBN 978 1 52944 475 9
EBOOK ISBN 978 1 52944 474 2

Typeset in Scala by CC Book Production

Printed and bound in Great Britain by Clays Ltd, Elcograf S.p.A.

MIX
Paper | Supporting responsible forestry
FSC® C104740
FSC www.fsc.org

Papers used by Quercus are from well-managed forests and other responsible sources.

Quercus
Carmelite House
50 Victoria Embankment
London EC4Y 0DZ

John Murray Group
Part of Hodder & Stoughton Limited
An Hachette UK company

The authorised representative in the EEA is Hachette Ireland,
8 Castlecourt Centre, Dublin 15, D15 XTP3, Ireland (email: info@hbgi.ie)

PART ONE

1

This morning a buzzard came shooting out of the sky and pounced on one of my young hens. She'd ventured out from the shelter of the fruit trees and started pecking away from the others. I was just pushing a barrow full of leaves, mud and dead branches past the chicken garden to the compost heap when, out of the corner of my eye, I spotted the bird of prey approaching. Letting go of the wheelbarrow, I yanked open the gate to the chicken garden and ran. Because I was wearing heavy-duty gloves I made a grab for the buzzard without thinking about it. With its short, curved beak it pecked at me, made high-pitched squawks and thrashed its wings wildly without letting go of its prey. The creature possessed a strength I hadn't expected, and I turned my head to the side to protect myself from its blows. When I'd got a proper grip on the buzzard I threw it back up into the air as hard as I could.

"Piss off!" I screamed in a voice that didn't sound like me.

For a moment it looked as if the bird was injured. Its wings didn't appear to be able to find their natural rhythm and it was floundering not far above me. Finally, however, with some powerful beats of its wings it rose up, circled once more above the chicken garden and finally flew away.

I remained there for a while, waiting to see if the buzzard would risk another attempt. My heart was racing; I could feel the blood pulsing into the tips of my fingers and toes. My breathing was loud and fitful, and at my feet lay the hen, not moving. Tearing off the gloves, I bent down and was just about to stroke her when she suddenly scuttled off as fresh as a daisy, leaving a few feathers on the ground.

For a moment I pictured my former self: the woman with the stylish hair, a partiality for cashmere, silk and expensive linen, manicured nails, eyes and lips always carefully made up, and an aversion to anything that was coarse or dirty. The hypochondriac who googled every symptom and always suspected cancer. The careful woman who threw away every item of food the day after its best-before date. The cleanliness obsessive who wiped and dusted after the cleaner had left.

With an instinctive shake of the head, I grabbed the wheelbarrow again, pushed it to the compost heap and emptied it. I turned the heap over with a pitchfork and scoured the sky for the bird of prey. Next time it would not escape unscathed. If it came back I'd smash its head with those rigid yellow eyes against the nearest tree.

My name is Linda.

Linda means *the mild one, the friendly one, the soft one.* This name has nothing to do with me.

It's still cold inside the house. The fire in the stove was lit only a few minutes ago. I'm wearing a long vest made of thick cotton, a roll-neck jumper and a padded gilet over it. The water for my tea is boiling. I drop some slices of ginger into it and place a wafer-thin one in my mouth. Then I put on some water for the potatoes and resist the urge to send Richard a message. I want to tell somebody about the buzzard and he's the only person I haven't driven out of my life.

Kaja won't leave my side. The dog senses everything and

reacts immediately. As I wander uneasily from room to room she stays close by me. The animal doesn't understand my behaviour; it makes her anxious. She wants a confident owner, whereas I'm sending out signals that confuse her and only increase her servile attachment.

I switch the radio on, sit at the table, start peeling the potatoes and tell Kaja to go to her bed beside the stove, which is now glowing with heat. She obeys at once. The forecast is for rain; the traffic report lists the road closures throughout central Germany in the wake of yesterday's storm.

It reminds me of an old GDR joke that makes me laugh out loud. Kaja lifts her head and looks at me in shock.

The wind has died down completely.

In the pallid winter light of this January day I'm sitting by the kitchen window, drinking fresh-ginger tea with a large dollop of honey and gazing outside. There's been no brightness. A uniform grey hangs over the area, swallowing all joy. It deadens every sensation, good as well as bad. I feel something, but this something won't come out. It's a small, inconspicuous and yet life-sustaining glimmer.

I remove the gilet and thick jumper. A pungent smell is coming from my armpits; I need to have a proper wash. The hair isn't so important; regular brushing is sufficient. I haven't used shampoo in ages. The sebum production regulated itself within a few months and my skin and hair seem healthier than before.

I crouch in the bathtub and turn on the shower tap. Hot briefly, then cold, then soap and a long rinse with cold water. After rubbing myself dry my skin is tingling and I feel warm. In the fogged-up mirror above the sink all I can see of my face is a blur. The fingers on my right hand trace the long scar the length of my collarbone. I rub ointment into it every day. It keeps the skin elastic and the purple-blue colour is gradually fading. Beneath this is where my thyroid used to be. It was destroyed by cancer and the doctors took it out to save my life. Their job is to save lives. They're not interested in the life they send the cured patient back to.

I didn't feel any of the fear or despair that often follow a cancer diagnosis. In truth I felt an odd elation, a sort of enhanced vitality in the face of death, and the feeling that a marathon runner must have shortly before the finish line. Richard, my mother and my friends couldn't believe it. Another blow after what had already happened. Why, they asked, why Linda, after everything she's been through?

Why not? I thought.

To me the cancer seemed to make perfect sense. My body had lost its ability to resist. For more than a year the grief had eaten its way through my cells. They'd been too weak. A logical course of events.

Richard did what men do when confronted with a crisis: find solutions. He spent entire nights researching online. He bought green tea, turmeric and broccoli because they're supposed to inhibit growth and kill off cancer cells; he banished sugar from the home and arranged doctors' appointments to get second and third opinions. The diagnosis remained the same.

A change took place in Richard that was clear to see. The dark weariness of recent months disappeared from his face, which had become haggard. The deep lines running from his nose to his mouth seemed to smoothen slightly and there was now a spring in his step. Finally there was a reason to leave the tragedy behind and get things done again. Fighting my cancer became his mission. Now it was time to move on.

By comparison my own fight wasn't a real fight, but simply a reflex triggered by the possibility of death. The killer by the name of Cancer placed its hands around the victim's neck and squeezed. The victim resisted instinctively, almost against her own will, for each creature resists death. The instinct for self-preservation is written into our DNA. Richard resented me thinking like this, for in this version of the story he didn't exist.

I think about Richard a lot. He's my husband – a good man from a friendly, functional family of children, parents, siblings, nieces, nephews and even two grandmothers, whereas my family consists almost solely of people who are dead and unknown. I chose him, this man who made up for my shortcomings, and, without being hypocritical, I can say that I love him.

Almost every day I ask myself if I'm being unfair on him. If I could do things differently, I would. Most people don't hurt others intentionally. They do their best, only their best is not good enough. Richard didn't do anything wrong either. He just turned around one day and looked forwards, while my gaze remained focused on the past.

When he visits he looks in silence at my now strong hands, makes remarks about my rigid discipline and about how I've discarded my vanity. The other day he watched me chop wood in the yard, the logs flying either side, then me chucking them into the wheelbarrow and later stacking them against the wall of the shed. His brow became knitted with faint lines. I could see just what a stranger I'd become to him.

A fire is now lit in the sitting room too. I push the wing-backed chair into the middle of the room and sit on it. Hanging on the wall facing the windows are pictures of the ancestors, children and grandchildren of Grete Adomeit, the previous owner of the house. I simply hung my pictures next to them.

Occasionally, especially late in the afternoon, I sit here and stare at the photographs until the onset of darkness blurs the outlines and eventually they vanish altogether. Then I sometimes hear Sonja, hear her voice quite clearly. *Mama*, she calls out, *Look, Mama*. Or she mutters to herself, lost in some game. I've also heard her voice from when she was a bit older. Mostly the voice gets quieter after a few seconds before disappearing completely. Sometimes it assumes a strange echo just before it fades to nothing, and each time I stop breathing and freeze, terrified of driving Sonja away with a careless noise. A single sound is enough to make her vanish. I have to be utterly still and then she'll stay. In these moments the dog pricks up her ears and almost always runs in the direction the child's voice is coming from.

2

Years ago we drove through this village. We'd only recently bought the car and this was our first outing in it. The car still smelled new and it was so clean that we all knocked the dirt off our shoes before getting in. Sonja sat in the back with headphones on, while Richard and I gazed out of the window as we drove at a snail's pace through the village because the traffic report had mentioned a speed trap.

"You wouldn't want to be buried here," Richard said, and I agreed.

It's a charmless linear village of two halves. In the southern half, old farms sit beside each other on either side of the busy road. Most of the gates are closed, the façades plain, and some display faded cloth banners with the words: ENOUGH IS ENOUGH! WE NEED A BYPASS NOW!

Old willows, some dead, line the edge of a dried-up village pond, the locked church is beginning to crumble, and newly planted lime trees stand on a broad strip of grass between the road and the houses. There must have been a time when the village was home to a lively market, the farmers selling their produce on either side of the road. These days nobody earns their living from farming anymore. The fields belong to some large, industrial agribusiness. In the mornings, the villagers open the gates, get into their cars, drive to work in the city, and return late in the afternoon with their shopping from the supermarket. They shut the gates and disappear. At night they close the blinds, and in the wan light of the street lamps all you'll see is a few cats prowling around and the odd fox. It's deserted during the day too; you don't see anyone walking along the well-maintained, wheelchair-friendly pavements that lead into the new village, where prefab stands beside prefab in garish colours, their gardens screened off with sheets of metal, gabions or concrete fences. Gravel and slate chippings in the front gardens, manure around the identical drought-resistant shrubs, trampolines behind the houses in areas laid to lawn with no flowers, where at night robot mowers cruise, severing the legs of hapless hedgehogs. Beneath the aluminium carports stand large vehicles with dark-tinted windows, like tanks hostile to all living things.

Nowhere is there less nature than in the new part of the village.

At the edge of this is the U-shaped complex of the home for disabled people, from where drivers pick up the residents in the mornings to take them to work or daycare in the nearest town.

Around the village the land is completely flat, parcelled into large fields with monocultures – oilseed rape and maize – wind turbines on the horizon, the occasional narrow strip of wildflowers, a legally prescribed ecological compensation area, a hedge, an old avenue of fruit trees with dying or already-dead trees, but no hill for miles around, nothing to catch and hold the eye.

During the day the traffic is non-stop. At night the roar of the vehicles does abate, but then there begins the drone of the planes, which gets louder and softer as they take off and land at the nearby cargo airport.

This is where I've been living for two years, a quarter of an hour's drive from the small town where I spent the first thirteen years of my life, and around forty minutes away from the flat in Leipzig which Richard still calls our home.

I met Grete Adomeit in the hospital grounds. She was sitting on a bench surrounded by a sprawling ornamental currant with shining pink fruits. I had arrived far too early for my check-up. The radioactive iodine treatment and my five-day quarantine, to avoid contaminating anyone around me, was over. I sat down beside the elderly lady. At the time I would often talk to complete strangers, people who knew nothing about me, who looked me in the eye without any sympathy or timidity, without embarrassment or the fear of saying something wrong.

Grete Adomeit had clamped her walking stick between her big thighs, her fingers on the handle. She was wearing a grey pinafore – a relic of GDR days – a cardigan missing two buttons, and opaque, skin-coloured tights that were laddered. She must have noticed me glancing at her ripped tights because now she looked at her legs too.

"Nothing's good quality anymore, it's all made to be thrown away."

Over the course of the half-hour wait before my appointment I learned that the woman, who was considerably older than eighty, lived on her own in a farmhouse in northern Saxony. Her husband had been dead for decades, while the two daughters both lived far away and weren't interested in the property or their mother. I heard that she had *creatures* and a dog and incurable cancer that would soon see her *in the ground*. She took a photograph from her handbag and showed it to me. A young man and woman looking serious in front of a large wooden door. Expressionless eyes gazed out from the woman's even, round face; in her hands was a bunch of lily-of-the-valley. The young man beside her had only one arm. He too was staring straight at the camera without the hint of a smile. Two of those who remained, driven together by necessity, was the thought that flashed in my mind.

Before I could ask if it was her wedding photograph, she said, "My farm. My house."

All her sentences were short, using only the most essential vocabulary. Presumably she seldom had the opportunity to talk and, as with any faculty that's out of practice, Grete Adomeit's power of speech had dwindled. She was worn out. The bleary eyes, the unkempt hair, most of which had fallen out, the shabby clothes, the dry, chapped hands and the amorphous body told of a hard life and a hard heart. I found her quite disagreeable.

I gave away little about myself. She couldn't understand what I did for a living, but her ears pricked up at one of my remarks. It must be comforting, I said, to have your own farm with a gate you can close and shut out the world. She looked askance at me, played with her dentures and frowned. As I got up to go, she let me know with some urgency a date and a time when she'd be sitting here again. She repeated the information twice, gripping my arm firmly.

On my way into the hospital building I could still feel the pressure of Grete Adomeit's strong fingers. Rubbing my forearm where she'd grabbed me, I tried in vain to play down the significance of the encounter.

I didn't mention Frau Adomeit to Richard; we barely spoke in any case. Since it had become clear that the cancer wasn't going to be the end of me, after school he would cycle straight to the studio he shared with a young female artist. He was painting again, even though he'd thought he'd never be able to. The young woman apparently always worked at night. He was already back home by the time she turned up, Richard reassured me several times, even though I'd never asked. A few years earlier this set-up would have made me feel uneasy; now, however, the idea just left me cold. The woman who was putting our marriage on the line was old and ill and went by the name of Grete Adomeit.

I was far too early for our next meeting, so found myself waiting on the bench. The date, time and place were correct; Frau Adomeit had repeated the information. I sat there and waited for ages, the appointed hour came and went, and I needed to go to the loo but didn't dare move from the bench for fear of missing the elderly lady. Eventually she arrived. She had a ponderous gait and moving was clearly painful; at every step she pushed the stick into the ground ahead of her and groaned.

She seemed to take it for granted that I'd waited. No apology or thanks issued from her lips. Instead she took a photo album from a dirty, worn cloth bag, handed it over and told me to leaf through it. It was the strangest album I'd ever seen. Only a few of the photographs featured family members; most were of the farmyard. A new fence, a wall with scaffolding, the inner courtyard with a young tree and a bench in front of it, neatly laid-out beds. Frau Adomeit named everything, tapping a finger on the pictures as if to make sure that nothing escaped my notice. She rapidly skipped over her husband and daughters.

"The girls don't want it," she gasped, making a dismissive gesture with her hands. She gave me a searching look, then asked, "Do you have a car?"

I told her I did, and before I could get to the bottom of this question Grete Adomeit stood up.

"Where is it?" she said, then started walking beside me with astonishing agility.

Early that evening I returned to an empty flat.

Richard came back late; I was lying in bed, having already taken my tablets. The Zolpidem was gradually working. I'd combined it with half a Mirtazapine, to avoid being awake again after a few hours. One of the side effects was that I forgot virtually everything that happened between taking the pill and the following morning. Which meant there was no point in talking to Richard now.

His cautious footsteps in the hallway went off towards the kitchen. By the time he joined me in bed I'd be fast asleep – motionless, dreamless, with gastric juices rising unhindered in my gullet, which would leave a burning pain in my chest the following day because the sedative prevented me from waking and swallowing. There's always a price to pay, I thought as I dozed off. The last thought I had was of Grete Adomeit and the seed of the idea she'd sown in my head.

Over the next few weeks I took regular trips to the village without telling Richard. Right from the start I sensed what a calming effect the place had on me. The forbidding façades, the empty pavements, the unimaginative front gardens, the bleak landscape – nothing stirred my feelings, nothing aroused my envy; none of the lives behind the walls and beneath the repulsively shiny roof tiles appeared desirable. But, most importantly of all, nothing reminded me of Sonja.

Not once here did I find myself staring at a slim, young woman with a high, bouncing ponytail, never did Sonja's face emerge from a group of young people, never did I hear her laughter in the street or see her bike leaning against a wall, nor were any of her friends suddenly standing beside me. She wasn't anywhere here and there was no corner behind which memories were lurking, ready to ambush me. Unlike in Leipzig, I was out of danger in this village. As far as Sonja was concerned I was in no man's land.

Grete Adomeit would walk me around the property, proudly presenting her sheep, chickens and vegetable garden, before serving some musty-tasting peppermint tea and she kept showing me the same old photos, while outside a dishevelled dog gazed longingly at the kitchen window from its hut.

It was colder in her kitchen than outside; it smelled of old people and sickness, of onions, frying oil and decay, and sometimes she would offer me some cake, which I graciously refused. When she'd had enough of me she said straight out that I should go; she didn't bother with pleasantries.

Each time I visited she was in worse health. Against the advice of her oncologist she'd refused any more treatment. The uterine cancer had spread to her bladder and bowel, and was now metastasising in other organs, in the tissue of her abdominal cavity and the surrounding lymphatic vessels. She would list the affected areas and appeared to be proud that she'd remembered them all. Every day she took strong pain-killers and spoke about her impending demise without any discernible regret. All she was worried about was the property and her *creatures*.

We agreed to sort other things out before she became too weak. Her daughters were happy with our plan. They didn't want to sell the property, but nor did they want to look after it. A tenant was the best solution for all concerned.

I told Richard only a few days before Grete Adomeit's death. Until the end I'd hoped that something would make me change my mind. In that case it would have been unnecessary to unsettle him with my deliberations. But there was no *deus ex machina* and I couldn't keep silent about my plan any longer.

I picked Richard up from school, then we walked in Clara-Zetkin-Park along the Elster flood channel, where the yellow leaves trickled down on us from the lime trees and glowed in the low-lying autumn sun. They fell like large golden coins as, without further ado, I told Richard that I was planning to move into the village. Just temporarily, to get some distance, to temper the pain that was always there and avoid the snares of memory.

He stopped and looked at me.

"Do I feature in your plans at all?"

"Yes," I said impulsively, "of course you do. It's just that . . ."

"Just that . . .?"

". . . that you're part of the problem."

"How so?"

"You're better, Richard. Your life is moving forward."

"I'm grieving too, Linda."

"Yes, but on a different level."

"And that's why you've got to move away."

I nodded; Richard shook his head.

"But that's nonsense!" he cried. "Surely you don't think you'll feel better all the way out in that village, in an old house!"

Leaning his bike against a tree, he took his phone from his pocket and googled the name of the village.

"You're mad!" he said. "The main road runs right through it! There'll be permanent traffic racing past your front door. And the planes fly over it, day and night. Are you nuts?"

"It's a thirty kph zone," I replied quietly, ignoring his fake laughter.

"Brilliant, Linda, absolutely brilliant. You'll feel really great there. You of all people!" He shook his head again. "You're out of your mind!"

Again I let the insult bounce off me without a word of protest.

"Look, I can see how you're gradually getting better," I said. "How happy you are when Ylvie or Arvid pop round, how you love playing with Ylvie's children. And I'm pleased for you. But I can't take it! I can't go out into the street without looking for our daughter. I stare at every blonde girl on a bike and each time my heart practically stops beating. Every place Sonja went in this city awakens images in my mind. Every street, every shop, every ice-cream parlour, every cinema. My pulse races, I can't breathe. I'm suffocating here, Richard!"

"Are you saying you'd stay if I was feeling worse?" he said.

"No . . . That's not it."

The sun had now disappeared behind the trees on the other side of the river, the trickle of yellow was finished and Richard said, "I don't know what else to say." Then he got on his bike and cycled off.

From then on it was no longer the paralysing stillness of grief that filled our flat, but a helpless silence.

Once he asked me, "Why can't you mourn *with me*?" I responded that this was like the favourite in a race asking the runner in last place why they didn't join them at the front. Another time I found him weeping at the kitchen table. Not realising I was there, he sobbed like a child, his elbows propped on the table, his face buried in his hands. When eventually he saw me standing in the doorway he looked at me in supplication. I ought to have given him a firm hug but I only had the strength for a brief rub of his shoulder.

And then there was the day when I got home from shopping and could hear the music from downstairs in the entrance hall. I recognised the song, one of the few Richard and Sonja could both listen to on those days we all used to clean the flat together; the two of them would sing along at the tops of their voices. I opened the door to our flat, went into the kitchen and put the shopping down. Richard, who was standing at the cooker, turned around. The expression of shock and guilt on his face removed the last of my doubts.

In the days that followed I checked my finances, spoke to the interim head of the art foundation who had been deputising for me since I'd been off sick, tendered my resignation – which was accepted slightly too quickly and gladly – and signed the rental contract for Frau Adomeit's house, for a year initially. For three hundred and fifty euros a month I would be living on the farmstead on the edge of the village, buildings on three sides, with sheep, chickens, a cat and an ugly dog who was called exactly as he looked: Shaggy.

I promised to keep the house in good condition, not undertake any refurbishments without the daughters' approval and let them know of any necessary repairs. Some of Frau Adomeit's furniture – those items they had an attachment to but didn't want in their own flats – I put into the empty barn, some things I kept in the house, and the rest was taken away. A short, friendly Syrian man with large bags beneath his eyes came past, looked at everything, took photos, made a rough estimate of how much junk there was and, after a brief calculation, quoted me a very reasonable price. He told me that he'd bought an old house too, in Thuringia, near Gera, and that his wife was taking great care of the garden but that the fig tree, which had been planted to remind them of home, had died last winter. Then he emphasised the reliability of his *boys* who were going to do the clear-out, explained that they spoke hardly any German, and asked if my husband and children were looking forward to moving here. When, after a short hesitation, I told him I'd be living here alone he let his sad, bleary-eyed gaze rest on me.

A local firm decorated the rooms, a neighbour took Frau Adomeit's sheep, the cat decided to switch owners, settling in with a young couple down the road, and then I moved into this house accompanied by the incomprehension of everyone who was still close to me.

From our flat I took only the essentials. Everything I needed fitted into two carloads. That morning Richard left the house shortly after seven as usual. Right to the end he'd refused to believe that I was really going to do this. When I went to give him a goodbye hug, he ducked out of it, pushed past me and said, "You really are nuts."

It was my childhood friend Esther who helped me with the move. Later she wandered through the sparsely furnished rooms of the cold house, staring in disbelief.

"This is death by instalments, Linda."

Richard rang three days after I'd moved out.

"I don't understand you," he said. "You're behaving like an animal that's gone off to die. But I'm here whenever you need anything. And I'll pop by regularly to check on you."

Nobody from my old life visits me anymore apart from Richard. Not even Esther. On my birthday and at Christmas I get friendly cards from her, telling me to get in touch. She says she'll always be there for me no matter how much time passes. I get regular postcards from my mother, too. The sayings on the front of the cards are a way around her own lack of words. *No matter how difficult yesterday was, you can always begin again today (Buddha). When the time comes that you could, the time has passed when you can (Marie von Ebner-Eschenbach). Encounters with people are what makes life worth living (Guy de Maupassant).* But here, in my third life, it's not people. It's animals and plants and the wind and the pictures of the dead on the walls.

3

The smell of chicken broth wafts through the entire house. Richard's coming to visit.

Every fortnight he interrupts the uniformity of my life for a few hours, bringing newspapers and magazines that he's finished with – they usually end up in the stove, unread – and a small surprise: a good cheese, a new recording of some Beethoven sonatas, a picture. Shortly before Christmas he came with a daylight lamp, which has been in my kitchen window ever since, replacing the sun I'm missing. He brings me greetings from our friends and his family, and asks how much longer I think I'll be using him as a bridge to the world. I shrug. He's right; that's exactly what I'm doing. I ask him to return the greetings and to reassure these people that it's got nothing to do with them – it's me, just me. I ask how those sending their greetings are getting on, without even entertaining the idea of getting in contact with them. They don't understand. They feel punished without having done anything wrong. Richard feels the same. Every fortnight he comes to this house, patiently hoping, and leaves a trace of himself behind. He creates tiny fragments of a common bond, but these won't be enough for a fresh start.

In the winter Richard keeps his visits short. The house depresses him, makes him restless; there's not a single room he feels comfortable in and he doesn't like going outside either. The walks around the village lack any charm and the wind blows permanently across the bare fields. I can understand Richard and never ask him to stay longer.

The days are so alike that, looking back, I can't distinguish between them. The prerequisite for remembering anything appears to be a minimum dose of something out of the ordinary, but my life here consists of rituals and routines that abolish all sense of time. I see no point in creating memories. Everything I wish to remember happened before Sonja's death.

Every morning I put on my greasy lambswool coat over my pyjamas, slip into some baggy tracksuit bottoms and lined wellies, and stomp over to the garden to let the chickens out, feed them and refill the nesting box. Out here in the country I'd expected large numbers of birds of all varieties, but some days I see nothing save for a few blue tits, great tits and sparrows. Blackbirds, woodpeckers and robins come occasionally, I've spotted nuthatches and greenfinches too, and once I saw a bullfinch. In the kitchen there's a bird identification guide that I consult whenever I encounter a new one.

After a strong coffee I go for a walk with the dog, who I've renamed, to the nearest wood, as far as the little stream which is dry except in winter. There and back it's a march of around an hour and a half. Frau Adomeit never took her for a walk. Kaja – formerly Shaggy – was her umpteenth dog and, like all the dogs in the village, always stayed on the farm. Kaja's entire training was based on her fear of Grete Adomeit's stick. As a kind new owner I immediately won Kaja's affection, but getting her to obey was hard work because I didn't have a stick, nor would I have been prepared to use one.

Afterwards I make breakfast: a porridge of oats or millet with pieces of apple, sunflower seeds and linseeds. Sometimes

I'm surprised by the care I take in making it. Part of me seems to want to stay healthy and strong.

Then I set about the necessary tasks in the house and garden, cooking and cleaning. It's astonishing how much there is to do all of the time. Thousands of little things that, when added up, fill every waking hour. After lunch I do some sudoku. Occasionally I doze off in the middle of it, falling into a short sleep full of dreams, which rarely lasts longer than half an hour. In the first few seconds after waking it's as if I have to learn everything from scratch again: who I was, who I am, why I'm here, what I've lost. The answers to these questions are like gut punches. Bent almost double I drag myself to the kitchen, fill the moka pot with water and coffee, and slowly, very slowly, I straighten up again.

I knit scarves and hats that nobody needs. I unravel them and start at the beginning again. I write memories of Sonja in a book before they're swallowed up by forgetting. I talk to Sonja, tell her everything, and all the answers lie in her permanent silence.

I listen to the ticking of the grandfather clock, the breathing of the dog, the creaking and groaning of the old house.

Then begins the long stretch between it getting dark and going to bed. Every chore is welcome. Wood in the stove needs to be replenished, dinner cooked, the washing-up done by hand, organic waste taken to the compost heap, more firewood fetched, dog hairs swept, chickens shooed into their hut, all doors and gates locked, towels rolled up and placed in front of the draughty windows. I'm never done. It doesn't exist, the moment when I look around and can't see anything more to do. My natural habitat was a compact city apartment, refurbished to a high standard and kitted out with all modern comforts. Here, by contrast, it's hard work, and hard work is good. So long as my hands keep moving, the thoughts don't churn in my head and I can survive the hours until bedtime. At half past nine I take the pills that reliably switch me off and free me from all pain for a few hours.

I put an empty pot on the cooker, balance a sieve on it and strain the chicken broth. The liquid is light brown with beautiful globules of fat. The rest remains in the sieve. I pick the chicken from the bones, toss it into the stock, add peas and carrots, and check the time. Richard's going to be here soon. You can set your watch by him. I seed a pomegranate, crack nuts, and thinly slice beetroot and a sour apple. As I mix all of this into a salad I say out loud, "Hello, Richard. Nice to see you, the food's almost ready." And immediately again, in a deeper, more confident voice, "Hello, Richard. Nice to see you. Sit down, the food's almost ready." I inspect my face in the tarnished bathroom mirror; I don't want him worrying about me.

His hands hold me a touch too tightly. I remain rigid until he lets go. He hangs his coat neatly on a hanger on the rack and curls his scarf around it.

To pre-empt his anxious How are you?, I tell the story about the buzzard, embellishing it a little, adding a touch of drama and savouring the new variant in which the buzzard returns to launch an attack on me. Richard listens in earnest.

"Unusual for a buzzard. Are you sure it wasn't a falcon?"

He takes off his glasses and rubs his eyes. I still find him attractive. There's something incongruous, mysterious about his face. His eyes are slightly too close together, in peculiar contrast to his angular chin and soft lips. Dimples appear when he smiles; when he puts on a serious expression he can look intimidating. But this impression is deceptive. He's a gentle man. They say the most dangerous person in a woman's life is her husband. But this is not true of Richard.

After we've eaten – he's had several helpings – he looks at all the photographs on the sitting-room wall.

"I don't understand why these pictures are still here. Why haven't you taken them down? I mean, those people aren't your family."

My gaze alights on Grete Adomeit's father, who is at the centre of the gallery. A stud keeper on a small East Prussian estate, an imposing man with a moustache and impeccable clothing. Beside him is a photograph of the entire family – the mother a whole head shorter than her husband, the children like organ pipes. The boys are in suits, the girls in pinafores with ruffles and all of them standing very straight, staring right at the camera.

"In the end all families are the same," I say. "They all have their living and their dead, their secrets and suffering, and nobody remembers whether this brief happiness frozen on camera was genuine or not."

"Ours was," Richard says.

He's aged. What happened has left its mark. Both of us knew that we'd never again be the same people, but we couldn't have any idea of who we would be and what we would look like. At the time my hair turned grey within three days. When I looked in the mirror a stranger looked back at me. It felt like a hostile takeover. As if I were still inside the person without ever being able to get back out.

Richard looks at me and I can see the question in his eyes. He hasn't asked it on his recent visits. Maybe he was afraid of my silence. Before that he'd modified it, defused it. Instead of "When are you coming back?" he'd say, "Are you coming back?" A Yes would mean that we had a future. But our future had been obliterated in a fraction of a second one humid July morning, shortly before a storm broke. A traffic light turned green, a seventeen-year-old cyclist with a blonde ponytail and loud music in her ears pedalled her racer, and a lorry driver who'd forgotten to check his wing mirror turned right across the cycle lane. Time stopped.

Richard's question is still hanging in the room. Are you coming back? It moves from my head to my stomach, but there is no answer anywhere in my body. Both of us look at the photographs; our arms are almost touching.

Grete Adomeit's pictures are static: all the subjects are standing bolt upright, their eyes fixed on the camera. They look serious, proud, dignified. Our photos have more colour, more laughter, more movement. Sonja as a little girl with red cheeks, wrapped up warm on a sledge; Sonja with her half-siblings Ylvie and Arvid amongst the wildflowers on Hiddensee; Richard and seven-year-old, gap-toothed Sonja on a houseboat in Brandenburg; Sonja as a baby with Ylvie and Arvid in the paddling pool; Sonja aged thirteen, having put make-up on for the first time; Sonja in a midnight-blue satin dress at her Confirmation; Sonja and I by a Bernini fountain in Rome, with a huge Dolce & Gabbana advert in the background; Sonja blowing out candles on her seventeenth birthday; Richard and Sonja hiking in the Elbe Sandstone Mountains; Sonja beaming at the party to celebrate the end of Year 11, arm in arm with her friends Freya and Lotte. My daughter's face is open, the tension has drained from her face after the difficult school year, her laughter pure, her eyes looking into the future. Three weeks later she was dead.

*

A sigh comes from deep inside Richard's chest. He looks at me warily and takes a step back.

"Linda, there's something I've got to tell you."

I know this phrase. Everybody does. The words are always the same; only the name before the comma is interchangeable. It's followed by an affirmation, a confession, which rarely results in the continuation of something.

What will be her reply? I think about myself. Will Linda skip this intermezzo and ask the only questions whose answers she's really interested in? Is it serious? Do you want a divorce?

But it doesn't work like that. Nothing can be skipped; everything has to be endured. And that's why she says, "I'm listening."

During his preamble she hides her impatience behind tightly clasped hands and a poker face. Surely she must understand that a life without hope and love is hard to bear, he says. She nods. His life is joyless, the loneliness intolerable at times, all alone in that huge flat. Another gentle nod. He met her at school. She was invited by the German department to read from one of her books and tell the students something about her life as a writer. Afterwards she popped into the staff room where she had a coffee, signed some books and chatted to his colleagues. And, yes, he was there too. He pauses for a moment while she imagines the initial glances exchanged between Richard and the writer. She's got two daughters, he continues. One has already left home, the other will soon be finishing school. He doesn't want anyone thinking he rushed into this purely for his own pleasure. He hasn't even slept with her yet. No, there's something else between them, a profound understanding, a love of art and something hopeful. Yes, something hopeful.

"What's her name and how old is she?" she now asks,

genuinely curious, as if they were talking about a different man and a different woman.

"Brida. And she's your age."

"Hmm," she says as if the name and age had made the whole thing clearer. She stands there oddly unmoved, beside him and the photographs of their past. But then it hits her. Her legs are trembling so badly she needs to sit down.

Richard goes over to the window and runs his fingers through his hair.

"May I remind you that you were the one who left? I've been living without you for two years!"

"I know."

"I lost Sonja too."

He turns to her. Something in his expression is unfamiliar; for a moment she struggles to breathe. There's no way I can lose him too, she thinks. She knows precisely what she ought to say now. That she loves him, needs him, and is going to come back. That there is hope.

"Shall we go for a little walk?" he says. "I could do with a bit of air and exercise."

Kaja seems to have understood him. She leaps up and wags her tail, but Linda doesn't fancy it. She can't deal with any details about Brida, the bringer of hope.

"I'll go then," he says.

She nods feebly. They go to the coatrack in the hallway; she takes the scarf and wraps it around his neck, as she's done so often in the past. A gesture from old times. He takes a step back and puts on his coat.

"I can't understand how you cope with living here," he says.

A short, silent embrace, then she's in the open doorway, watching him walk to the gate.

*

I'm enveloped by total silence inside the house. A suspicious silence that feels familiar. I close my eyes, pause for a moment and then the whistling begins in my left ear, getting slowly louder. It ratchets up higher and higher, eventually levelling out at an unpleasant frequency. With the sound comes the leap of memory. How many more times, I wonder, will I have to experience this?

I was tormented by tinnitus that morning in the summer holidays too, as Sonja and I were having a late breakfast at the kitchen table. A few weeks earlier she'd fallen in love with Niklas, also seventeen, same school, same year, studying maths and physics. She was chatting about this and that, and the name Niklas cropped up in almost every sentence. The high-pitched buzzing in my head had begun shortly after I'd got up and I was finding it difficult to listen to her. Like her friends, Sonja spoke at a speed that made it impossible to entirely understand what she was saying. A constant stream of words without punctuation. I switched off for a while, nodding occasionally, giving an acquiescent Hmm, and then I interrupted her with a conspicuous glance at my watch: "Don't forget your appointment with the gynaecologist."

Another torrent of words disgorged over me, and I learned how Lotte, Freya, Lisa and Nike were faring since they'd started taking the pill. The noise in my ear rose in volume, but then came the sentence that actually silenced the tinnitus for a few seconds.

"I won't have to die a virgin now."

"Why do you think you're going to die?"

She smiled and shrugged, replying with that nonchalance typical of young people, which stems from the certainty of having an endless amount of life ahead of them: "You can die any day, Mama."

I got up and started clearing the table. I didn't respond to her comment. All I said, to dispel the horror of the idea, was: "Don't forget your medical insurance card! And take a raincoat. A storm is on its way."

"Yes, yes," she said, irritated.

And then she did die. A virgin. Beneath the wheels of a lorry. Seventeen years old.

Everything since stems from this. It sits at the centre of my existence like a black hole, swallowing every future before it can begin.

Of course things did happen *afterwards*, but they were insignificant. Everything that occurred revolved around this moment. Every thought returned to it, every feeling was born from it. There was nothing, absolutely nothing, that wasn't related to it. Even today there's nothing, absolutely nothing that I can view in detachment from it.

Sonja didn't suffer; she was unconscious and died in the ambulance. This is what the doctor told us when we arrived at A & E. Just before that, as we were parking the car at the hospital, the sun had broken through and I'd interpreted this sudden brightening of the cloudy sky as a good sign. I ran on ahead, grabbed the first doctor I could find and asked where we needed to go. Right after that I was intercepted by another doctor who asked our names, made sure that we were Sonja's parents, took us into a consultation room, invited us to sit down and closed the door gently. The expression on her face wasn't encouraging and she didn't keep us guessing for another second.

"I'm so very sorry, but I'm afraid your daughter didn't survive the accident."

Richard leaped to his feet and I shouted, "No, that's not possible." Then I asked, "Where is she?" and tried to catch

Richard's eye. But all I could see on his face was sheer horror and at that moment I realised that our life as we knew it was over. My perception changed at a stroke. Although the man paralysed by shock looked like Richard, the Richard from our former life had already left the room. Every object, the light, the air, the sun breaking through and casting its rays onto the doctor's desk, looked like the things they used to be, but now they belonged to a completely different universe. This new universe contained everything that had existed in the old one, only without the happiness or insouciance.

"Where is she?" I asked again, but in truth I was screaming the words. I got up and yelled, "Where is Sonja? I want to see her!"

The doctor's calm, firm gaze was now on me. She seemed to be weighing up her answer, then said, "I'll take you to your daughter in a minute. But beforehand I'd like to tell you what's going to happen next."

"Stop!" I cried. "Stop! Stop! Stop! Nothing's going to happen. Not without Sonja!"

Richard hugged me so tightly that I couldn't breathe. He squeezed me until I pushed myself away and gasped for air. Then we sat down and listened.

4

I've just had a night without pills. Eight hours of a racing heart, sweating and circling around thoughts until they became monstrous. Every thought becomes menacing in the hours between midnight and dawn. I wanted it to be like this. I wanted to drain the cup to the dregs. The pills were within reach; all I had to do was take them. Instead I imagined Richard and the writer, their naked bodies in our bed, having breakfast together at our kitchen table, Brida wandering through our flat, going down the corridor with all the artworks we've collected over the years, her secret peek into Sonja's empty room. I saw Richard coming naked out of the bedroom, wearing the satisfied expression of a man who at last is being desired once more.

At daybreak I must have nodded off briefly. I had an absurd dream about Richard and Sonja, and as I gradually surfaced from the depths of unconsciousness I had a vision. The second child, the one who'd never been born, came to my bed and laid its hand on my head. I closed my eyes, hoping it would disappear. But the tall, slim, translucent figure came closer.

"Why were you never born?" I whispered, and it answered, "You know why."

When I get up I know that the day is lost. My limbs are aching and every thought leads into the darkness. I haul myself into the bathroom, get dressed, see to the chickens, fill Kaja's bowl with food, make some tea and take it to the bedroom, where I close the curtains and crawl back under the covers. I want to switch off the thoughts and sink into nothingness, but my memory leaps back to the beginning again, and the bizarre hope that I might be able to intervene retrospectively and change the course of events makes me live through all the possibilities once more.

It was the end of April, at the spring tour of the galleries at the Alte Baumwollspinnerei, the old cotton mill. Richard was there with his children. Ylvie and Arvid were larking about with other children in the huge space while their father was sitting under an umbrella, drinking white wine and talking to another man. We sat opposite them – I was there with my friend, a freelance curator like me. It was unusually warm for the end of April, I'd got dressed up and was wearing a loose-fitting, dark-green silk dress, ruby earrings and matching lipstick. I could sense the men opposite looking at me and I gave them both a smile. Arvid, whose name I didn't yet know, came racing over and leaped onto his father's back. Grabbing hold of the boy, Richard lifted him onto his lap and hugged him tightly.

"The good ones are always spoken for," my friend whispered.

We got talking to Richard and Hauke – a deep, serious conversation, none of the small talk you usually have at such events. We spoke about men and women, relationships, love and what it can withstand. When it came to the question of the nature of masculinity, Richard asked my friend and me what we thought.

"Protection!" we cried in unison, and looked at each other in shock.

"Agency," Richard said.

"Initiative," Hauke added.

"Good God, what century are we in?" my friend said, then heretically she asked the counter-question.

"Communication!" I cried first. "Multitasking," Hauke said. My friend settled for "Beauty", visibly disgruntled that she couldn't think of anything better to say about femininity. Only Richard said nothing. Hauke briefly put a hand on his shoulder, but the conversation no longer flowed. The mood had changed; my friend and I moved on.

A few weeks later I saw him again at a finissage, this time without his children. He cocked his head slightly when he saw me and, when he was certain he'd recognised me, smiled, waved and came over.

I had his undivided attention. When he spoke his eyes remained fixed on me, not straying to any other women; he gazed at me alone. I want children with this man, I thought. Not *a* child. I was thinking in the plural right from the beginning.

We filled our glasses and stepped out into a cold, starry spring night. Richard smoked and I took a few puffs of his roll-up. I asked him outright why he hadn't been able to say anything about femininity when we'd met at the gallery tour. He gave me a searching look.

"A few things did come to mind, but I didn't fancy talking about them with two women I didn't know."

Before I could probe further he suggested we move on to somewhere else. We cycled to Besser Leben, where we ordered two small beers, and then he told me about Marianna. They'd separated about a year earlier, having known each other since college. Both had studied painting and were part of that generation of young artists, some of whom had achieved worldwide fame under the New Leipzig School label. Richard and Marianna had had children and they'd packed away their great dreams into the little drawers of everyday life. Bread-and-butter jobs, sleepless nights, difficult conversations about who would have how much time for their art when.

"She wanted to have children but not look after them," Richard said softly.

And then, during an argument one day – later he couldn't have said who'd begun it – she hit him. He didn't get out of the way because, until her hand actually made contact with his face, he didn't believe it was going to happen. But it did. And it happened again. The third time, he knew that he would hit back if it came to a fourth. He left Marianna that same day.

"Maybe now you understand why I didn't have an immediate answer to what constitutes 'femininity'." He smiled. His beer remained untouched; the head on it had already disappeared. "She hates me," he added, "because I didn't hit her back."

But I loved him for it. At that very moment in Besser Leben, when he finally took a sip of his beer and looked at me sceptically, I loved him for his self-control; it hadn't had anything to do with fear, but with the willpower to maintain a boundary that can only be justifiably crossed in the most extreme circumstances. He was perfectly able to fight back, as I witnessed years later when we were taking a walk in the woods and a large dog leaped at Sonja, barking aggressively. In a flash Richard grabbed a stick and thrashed the dog as forcefully as he could before it could harm our child. "Have you lost your mind?" the owner screamed. Richard replied calmly that he should put his badly trained mutt on a lead.

After the evening in Besser Leben I visited him regularly in his studio. Rammstein were usually playing, though Richard's pictures couldn't be more different to the band's violent lyrics. His art was reserved and explored the question of what masculinity still meant in the modern Western world. The theme came from that violent episode with Marianna; on canvas Richard processed his pain, anger and disbelief. His figures stood isolated and bent in arid woodland, sat on rocks or peered out of tiny attic windows at overgrown gardens where, on closer inspection, climbing plants turned out to be the outlines of women's bodies. A voluptuous female nude with an angular, almost masculine face, was one of his strongest works. Contrary to all the feminist noise, society wasn't developing in a feminine direction as far as he was concerned, but becoming unhealthily more masculine because women were aping male characteristics instead of confidently confronting the masculine with their femininity. Thus began a conversation that didn't stop until the day our daughter died. I'd arrived, I was at home. But this harbour had already been headed for by a woman whose name was known in the local art scene, whose attractiveness was irrefutable, and whose alliance with Richard had produced two children. Almost all the problems that would be inflicted on me derived from the simple fact that I was the second.

I practised being a mother before I had my own child. Ylvie and Arvid came to visit their father every second Thursday afternoon and would stay until the following Tuesday. Sometimes Marianna also arrived unscheduled with the children, on a spontaneous whim that Richard always tolerated, much to my annoyance. He loved the children; any extra time with them was a gift. These days almost always followed the same pattern: Marianna would chuck the children's bags at our feet on the doorstep, bark a few instructions and rush off without saying goodbye. Ylvie would run into the entrance hall, where she'd either throw herself melodramatically on the floor or stand facing the wall. Arvid would have a face like a wet weekend and shoot me accusatory looks. Once we were inside the flat the two children would demand Richard's mental and physical attention. Whenever he put an arm around me one of the children would immediately butt in and throw themselves on him. Fighting the antipathy I felt towards them, I played with the children, cooked their favourite dishes, feigned joy when they arrived and sadness each time they left.

There wasn't even any peace at night. They squeezed themselves between us, pushed me over and then snuggled up either side of Richard while, stuck at the very edge of the bed, I tried to avoid any contact with them. Whenever Richard reached over one of the children to restore the disrupted connection between us, I pretended to be asleep.

I wished I could have loved these lively, beautiful, strong children, but I found it hard to tolerate them. Some days, everything about them annoyed me – the way they ate, spoke, charged around the flat, smelled, forgot to flush, naturally monopolised Richard's body, clambered all over him, hung from his arms and legs. I had to look away; I could barely stomach it.

I wanted my own children as quickly as possible and always spoke about this in the plural to Richard too.

"How about we start with one first," he would then say softly, but I felt that his words were entertaining the idea of a second.

During my pregnancy I temporarily liked the idea that my children would already have two older siblings and I tried more than ever to strengthen my relationship with Ylvie and Arvid. I let them put their hands on my tummy to feel the baby moving and asked them what they felt when they thought about the baby.

"Love," Ylvie said.

"Dunno," Arvid said.

But as soon as Sonja was born my interest in Ylvie and Arvid vanished almost completely. They were a necessary evil I had to put up with in a fourteen-day cycle, and it took all of my energy to avoid them sensing this. Only an emergency brings out the truth in people, and all the time I hoped I wouldn't get into a situation where it became obvious what I really thought of them.

During Sonja's first year, Richard plunged into a crisis. He could scarcely paint anymore and, in his pedantic attempt to be fair to everyone, he lost his patience more and more often. He cursed when something fell over, yelled at the children if they didn't appear the moment he called and groaned irritably whenever I gave him another shopping list as he left the flat. None of this prevented me from reminding him about the second child, who as far as I was concerned was going to follow on speedily.

In those early months, however, even I wasn't as half as delighted with the baby as I'd expected to be. Everything that Sonja did for the first time, Richard had already been through with Ylvie and Arvid – the first smile, gripping things, rolling over, then teeth and the first solid food, sitting up and crawling. His first children had already exhausted his sense of wonder and curiosity. They'd established the order in which I would always be the second wife and Sonja the third child, even though both he and Sonja would take first place for me. This was irrevocable and trying to fight it was hopeless.

To Richard's irritation and my restlessness, Ylvie and Arvid began to misbehave. They were insolent, loud and moody.

Their mother never laid down any hard-and-fast rules, changed her lovers regularly, allowed the children to be looked after by too many babysitters, and she had an alcohol problem. Barely a day went by without a new drama and yet I wanted to get pregnant again as quickly as possible. Richard thought I was crazy. It would be too much for us in terms of space – psychologically, physically and materially. My second child would be his fourth, did I realise that? If he had four children he might as well give up painting for good. Even now he scarcely had time for it. Our flat was too small, Marianna's behaviour unpredictable – no, no way, absolutely not.

But my desire was stronger than any reservations. It came from the depths of my soul, brushing every argument aside. On the day of Sonja's birth when, happy and exhausted in a bed at the Elisabeth Hospital, I first fed my daughter, my mind was already on the second child. Many years later, after Sonja's death, the old gut feeling combined with the new reality and finally made sense.

But interpreting backwards doesn't help one to go forwards in life – it didn't then and it doesn't now – and at the time I had no explanation for the burning desire inside me. I did everything to undermine the foundations of Richard's resistance and bring it crashing down. I insisted, demanded, begged, didn't give a damn about my dignity, but the only thing that I achieved was that Richard stopped sleeping with me. He increasingly withdrew into himself and in some moments seemed almost to be scared of me. The *brute force of my will*, as he put it, was almost as violent as Marianna's blows. It was the most terrible and, at the same time, effective accusation he could level at me.

I gave up for the time being and went back to the museum after nine months. The person covering my maternity was unwell and they were pleased by my apparent flexibility, which was nothing more than an escape. Richard stayed at home with Sonja for another three months and then helped her settle into daycare. He'd rehearsed this role with Ylvie and Arvid and took it on unquestioningly, in the belief that I'd be pleased.

A few weeks after I'd gone back to my job, in the midst of preparations for the retrospective of an important artist from the city who'd recently died, I confronted him again. To organise the loans of the painter's works, which were scattered around the country, I worked overtime, often coming home late. On one of those evenings I told Richard that it was still my greatest wish to have a second child. I was sitting in the kitchen; he was in the doorway brushing his teeth. He looked at me as if I'd lost my mind. Then he went to the sink, took the toothbrush from his mouth, spat and said curtly, "No."

For a while I focused on his older children again, trying to be a good stepmother. Although I hate board games and cards, for whole evenings I pretended to Ylvie and Arvid that I was a big fan of Monopoly, Cluedo or Uno, in the hope of shattering Richard's resistance with the proof of my perfect motherhood. But he stuck with his No.

For a long time I would stare at every mother with more than one child. The envy shot through me like the thrust of a dagger.

Sonja learned to walk, speak, draw and count, and I became calmer. After Richard had forced a promise out of me not to abuse his trust, we slept together again, and often. He knew cases of "finagled children" and found such behaviour unforgivable. He'd seen through me.

Our life fell into a routine. Richard spent three mornings a week painting in the studio; the rest of the time he worked in the shop belonging to his friend Hauke, who restored prints and sold made-to-measure frames. Not only did he pay Richard a fair wage, he also gave him a share of the profit on big, lucrative commissions. When Sonja was three I moved to a considerably better-paid job, looking after a bank foundation's extensive art collection. Our life was good. We were healthy, privileged, leading a secure, affluent existence. While many couples around us were separating and forming new, complicated patchwork families, we bought a flat. We came up with three quarters of the capital ourselves and the rest we borrowed. Richard's parents gave him an interest-free loan and my stepfather gave me and my half-brothers an advance on our inheritance. My management job in the foundation was very varied. I had a six-figure annual acquisition budget and, instead of archiving, database management, looking after the inventory and renting out the foundation's rooms, which I did in later years, I travelled to art fairs, visited studios, exhibition openings, auctions and viewed collections of unexhibited works by local artists. At the time we couldn't have predicted that the policy of low-interest rates would soon lead to a zero budget, and that I would once again have to do the work of the full-time assistant I'd been able to employ to relieve me of the lion's share of bureaucracy. Professionally it was the high point in my life; the work didn't feel like work, more like a generously remunerated hobby. I was doing what I enjoyed, my husband was doing what he enjoyed and we had a wonderful daughter.

Only rarely did the old pain resurface. During our annual summer holiday on Hiddensee, surrounded by all the happy summer faces and carefree nakedness in the dunes between Kloster, Vitte and Neuendorf, when some random woman sunbathing next to us looked over and said, "Three beautiful children and you look so young." An anxious glance from Richard, a serious expression on Arvid's face. "That's not my mummy." Richard, looking away, Ylvie frowning at me and my friendly, unnecessary explanation: "Only the little girl is mine." I would leap to my feet, hurry barefoot across the beach, breathing steadily to allay my agitation, and finally plunge into the cold Baltic. Submerge. Feel the almost painful tingling. A silent scream underwater. It was here that I felt the curative effect of the cold for the first time.

Sonja turned four, five and six. She was able to write her name, ride a bike, add up to twenty, do perfect cartwheels, ski better than all of us and somersault on the trampoline. She showed everyone her front and side splits, was friendly, helpful and, according to her grandparents, what you would call an "easy child". No behavioural issues, no serious illnesses, good results in the school entrance tests.

We were a happy family.

One summer's day by Kulkwitzer See, when Sonja was about to start school, Richard said something that crashed into this happiness. While Sonja was playing with her toy animals in the shallow water by the lake's shore and looking over at the diving students, vanishing one by one into the depths of the lake, Richard suddenly sat up, adjusted his Panama hat and said, "Do you still want another child?"

I stared at him, briefly thinking I'd misheard.

"Another *child*?" I echoed. From my lips the words sounded so alien, as if I'd said dog or cat.

The roguish smile had already disappeared from Richard's face. "Yes, a *child*," he repeated, quieter this time.

I couldn't believe what I was hearing. It had taken me years to come to terms with the fact that Sonja would remain my only child, and now, as casually as you like, he was opening the locked door to which only he had the key. He gestured to Sonja, who was absorbed in her game now that the divers had finished.

"We could raise another one of those."

"One of *those*?"

"She's so uncomplicated. So different to how Ylvie and Arvid were at that age."

I was lost for words. As if all the wrangling, the endless discussions, the sleepless nights, the mistrust, arguments and tears had never happened.

"Let's talk about it some other time," he said. "I didn't know you'd get so worked up about it. I thought you'd be pleased."

I hated him just then. That morning we'd been happy. He must have thought he could have enhanced this happiness. Instead he'd destroyed us. He'd thrown us abruptly out of step, interrupting our harmonious dance.

The anger boiled in my stomach, producing a pressure that would have erupted there and then had it not been for the other people on the beach and our daughter playing peacefully. With her infallible sensibility to mood changes she now looked over at us. I hastily packed up our things, hissing words at Richard that I'd have loved to scream in his face.

"This is YEARS too late . . . The baby would grow up like a grandchild . . . Sonja's about to start school . . . Ylvie and Arvid are on their way to becoming adults . . . Why now? . . . It would turn EVERYTHING upside down."

All the way back I cycled so far ahead of Richard and Sonja that a conversation was impossible. We spent the rest of that sweltering day in the apartment, where we avoided each other, only speaking to Sonja. Only when Sonja spotted from the balcony two girls from our neighbourhood and soon vanished into the labyrinth of courtyards bordered by hedges and trees, did Richard bring the subject up again. He didn't feel the urge to have another child himself, he said; he was thinking of me. As far as he was concerned our life was fine as it was, almost perfect.

I didn't know what to say. We were still the same family that had cycled cheerfully to the lake that morning, but now everything was bathed in a different light.

For weeks I weighed up the pros and cons, without being able to reach a conclusion. We knew many families with just one child and all of them seemed to be getting along fine. None of these couples seemed to regret not having had another. They looked less stressed, healthier, had more disposable income and could offer more to their child than parents who had more than one. The only condition was that nothing must happen, everything depended on that.

It took me months to come to a decision. I used the most rational of arguments to subdue the old instinct inside me. I cancelled my gynaecologist's appointment to have my coil removed. Occasionally a translucent, sexless being would enter my dreams, but at some point it would vanish as suddenly as it had appeared.

It's almost midday and I'm still lying in bed. Kaja keeps coming in, stands by the bed, makes a few noises then trots off again. These have been wasted hours. I'd hoped to be able to doze off again, but I didn't get anywhere close to sleep. It would be wise to eat something now, so I get up and go to the kitchen. I cut myself a thick slice of bread, toast it, then spread it with butter, almond butter and jam. Kaja's delighted; she thinks it's all going to kick off now. But I'm not yet finished with myself, Sonja, and the second child who was never born.

It's as if this day was made for diving into the past, so I plod back to bed and sink once more into my memories. The dog understands. She turns around a few times on the bedside rug, then curls up with her muzzle pointing at my pillow.

I close my eyes and summon images of my daughter. They fade by the week, and one day Sonja's substance will be lost too, her contours will blur and every attempt to recall them will end in a cursory fog.

I loved my daughter more than anything in the world and yet I was disappointed by her.

In the company of her siblings, Sonja came across as ordinary. She looked like Ylvie, but lacked her presence. Sometimes I thought she appeared like a paler, thinner version of her sister, a shadow-Ylvie, and I hated myself for thinking this. She was attentive and helpful, sociable, empathetic. Richard called her "porous", and when he said it there was concern in his voice. He knew what it meant because he was porous himself, someone who sensed things that remained concealed to others. Someone who had a hunch about events before they happened, and whose predictions usually came true. He didn't have any supernatural powers, he merely perceived things with the greatest of precision.

Sonja had nothing in common with Arvid, who she followed around like a dog. From the very beginning I found him sinister. There was nothing sweet about this boy. His face was that of an old man and his expression mature and knowing. He didn't say much, but the way he looked! He resembled Richard's father, apparently, and this was confirmed by the few childhood photographs that existed of my father-in-law. I hated being able to see the bloodline come through so clearly in Arvid, as it didn't manifest externally in Sonja. He took the adulation without paying her much attention. Although Arvid didn't stop her following him, he barely included her in his games, which were anyway best played alone. Making fragile towers from KAPLA wooden blocks, puzzles and role-play fighting invisible opponents were things he could do better than Sonja, and unlike her he never got bored. If he'd had enough of her presence he simply pushed her out of the room and gently shut the door. She would lurk behind it, waiting, and the mere sight of this brought tears of anger to my eyes. My fury was aimed less at Arvid's behaviour than at Sonja's devotion, her weakness.

She was incapable of doing something to her own advantage and couldn't cope with any friction or discord. When Richard and I argued, when things got heated, her eyes radiated sheer terror. We made every effort to teach her that conflict was part of life, that people spoke more harshly when they argued, and that this was neither bad nor dangerous if apologies were exchanged afterwards. But her sunny disposition resisted this, wanting peace at any price.

At school she floated in the middle. Only in sport did she exhibit the potential for high achievement, though she never lived up to this. Ambition was alien to her. She would usually dash off her homework half-heartedly and was satisfied with test results even when they were mediocre. If I asked her what she liked about school, she'd say, "Break times, because I can play with my friends." Sonja never stood out, neither in a negative or positive way. Sometimes she suffered from the noise in the classroom; she would put her hands over her ears and cry. Sometimes she was sad because she often put her hand up but was seldom chosen. What she wanted most of all was to belong. The compromises she struck for this were often significant, but almost everybody liked her.

By contrast, Ylvie and Arvid were children with solid centres. With characters that could be clearly described, brimming with strength, willpower and conviction.

Ylvie hardly ever compromised. Not as a child, nor later either. She would accept punishment and exclusion to be able to continue defending her point of view. Arvid was more malleable, a strategist, manipulative and successful with this approach. Time and again he formed advantageous alliances, skilfully playing me against Ylvie when he noticed how much she annoyed me sometimes. This created a bad atmosphere between Richard and me, and gave Arvid more time with his father. The boy was gifted too. Before he even started school he was drawing pictures that nobody would think had been done by a child: a leaping tiger, a dinosaur turning its head backwards and opening its jaws. And everything about these drawings was correct: proportion, perspective, light and shadows. In his last year at school, Arvid applied to various art colleges and they all offered him a place.

In the middle was Sonja, who had no special talents and was trying to please everybody all of the time.

Physically, Sonja developed later than most of the other girls in her class. Whereas Ylvie looked like a fully grown woman at the age of fourteen, and behaved like one too, Sonja hadn't even started her periods by that age. She was tall and as thin as a rake. Ever since she was five, once she'd realised that a chicken had to die to make crispy drumsticks, she hadn't eaten meat. A year later, during a winter holiday on a farm in the Allgäu, she refused to drink milk from one day to the next. The farmer had shown her where the calves were kept and explained why they weren't able to stay with their mothers. Sonja was horrified by the idea that she could only have her daily hot chocolate and porridge because a cow had its calf taken away. So we bought substitute products and an arsenal of food supplements that Richard was mainly responsible for ensuring she took.

Sonja's sensitivity made me furious. I found it absurd that something so basic as eating could have become a problem. All those artificial drops and powders we gave Sonja daily were expensive, and administering them at the right time and in the right dose required our permanent vigilance. The paediatrician brought up eating at every consultation. Sonja weighed too little, she said, she was too pale, had insufficient muscle tone. Whenever we visited my mother and Konrad in Kronberg, we'd hear the inevitable sayings. "You can see right through her. That girl's just skin and bones. She needs a proper hunk of meat!" Richard's parents in Weimar weren't short on advice either and they tried little tricks: tomato sauce was thinned with beef stock, rice cooked in chicken stock, porridge enriched with cream. Richard's father called Sonja's eating habits "finickity" and "a middle-class fad". His mother no doubt felt the same, but she stifled her comments.

Usually we'd bring Ylvie and Arvid with us to Weimar. Ylvie in particular, who ate everything without exception, was frequently praised for her "good appetite", and I bravely swallowed my anger. When Ylvie got married at nineteen and had her first child soon afterwards, Richard's father said about the chubby little boy at her breast, "He already weighs more than Sonja."

Sonja took no offence at any of this, however. She loved her half-siblings. I was never allowed to call them that. She would correct me by saying "my sister" and "my brother". She was a kind-hearted soul, and I feel ashamed of every moment when I wished my child was anything different to how she was.

*

The cold is stealing through the bedroom and under the duvet. My feet, chest and back are covered in cold sweat, my teeth are chattering and hunger is gnawing away at the walls of my stomach. I can see Kaja lifting her head and opening her mouth. *Get up,* she seems to be saying, *it's high time you got up.* I do so and trudge shivering into the bathroom. I see all the ugliness, the cracked sink, the yellowed bathtub, the dripping tap. Not everything old is beautiful; some things are merely old and worn out. The dog follows me and stands in the doorway, wagging her tail. *Pull yourself together,* my mother would say now. *Pull yourself together,* I mutter to myself, *come on, have a wash, clean your teeth, go for a walk with the dog.* Turning the showerhead to the hard massage jet, I let ice-cold water crash against my body, working up from my feet. The cold separates my soul from my body, freeing it from pain. The longer I expose myself to it, the clearer my thoughts become, the more vigorous I feel, and the more incomprehensible I find the pitiful woman who's spent half the day in bed. In the few hours that remain until darkness falls I actually manage to believe that I might be able to rise above my suffering.

5

It's just after six o'clock and still dark outside. Richard won't be coming back for a fortnight. Nobody would find me if I were to end my life now. This thought gives me satisfaction; I think it again and again, imagining myself lying on my bed, wrists slashed, having bled to death.

Kaja barks, which she never usually does. Her body is almost bursting with tension. She trembles, races to the door and stands there, whimpering. She keeps turning to me, running over, pressing herself against my legs, then going back to the door. I quickly finish my coffee and get dressed.

A cold front has arrived overnight. Blinded by the sun, which has been in hiding for weeks and is now far too bright, I hurry along the zigzag path between the fields to the woods. An icy eastern wind whistles around my ears and I pull my hat down. The dog trots obediently at my side. Later we meet forestry workers, clearing the storm damage. Their chainsaws squeal in the young day. It doesn't interest Kaja. With her nose close to the ground she's sniffing out the dung and traces of other animals, while the smell of freshly sawn wood awakens a sudden memory in me.

It was Sonja's first day on earth. When Richard brought us home from the hospital, I noticed how the light in our kitchen had changed; it was brighter than usual. With Sonja in my arms I went over to the window. The large pine tree had gone. For the first time I could see the whole of the building opposite, whereas before it had been screened by the pine. The exposed building stood there as if unmasked, vulnerable and subject to the nosy gaze of its neighbours. They were able to look over at us for the first time too, watch us in the evening through the lit-up windows, notice whether we were in or out.

For the rest of the day, the joy of having my new baby was accompanied by a feeling of loss. I was pleased to have missed seeing and hearing the men opening the crown of the old tree with their howling chainsaws, then taking the trunk down bit by bit all the way to the stump. The smell of wood still hung in the air and was intermittently brought into the flat. Sonja's arrival and this spicy tang have been inextricably linked ever since.

My footsteps automatically speed up. The icy winter air is burning inside my lungs. I return to the house half an hour earlier than usual, feed the dog, put on my porridge and wish Grete Adomeit could be here with me for a short while. "The only thing that helps is work," she said to me on one of our first meetings. She left it at that, without being more precise, and I see the truth of these words every day. Work saves you from loneliness, grief, negative thought spirals, the feeling of meaninglessness, sleeplessness and fear. The simpler the work the better. Adding to the verbosity of this world – or trying to counter it – with more words is pointless. A swept courtyard or a blooming garden, on the other hand!

A message from Richard. *When you know what you want, let me know. I'll always be there for you, in one way or another. See you in a fortnight. R.*

I don't reply.

*

After my lunchtime rest I have a coffee, put on my watch and check the other clocks in the house – the wall clock in the kitchen and the grandfather clock in the sitting room. I need to keep track of the time because this afternoon I'm expecting visitors. Nina's coming past with her mother. I often hear the girl from a distance. She lives at the edge of the village in the home for disabled people. As she walks along, Nina's bright and pure voice rings out. Whenever the dog and I greet her at the door she looks at me with her large blue eyes, gently puts her index finger to my lips and starts singing that song I sang to her when we first met. Her carer had told me that Nina wasn't able to speak and only reacted to music.

In Nina's presence Kaja is transformed into a different, shrewder creature. You can see the enhanced watchfulness in her eyes. She stays close to Nina the whole time, loves to lie at her feet, and if Nina sits on the floor – which she often does – Kaja will rest her muzzle on her legs. It was the dog who established the initial contact on one of our walks. Kaja brought Nina to my house.

Shortly before four o'clock Kaja and I are at the gate, looking down the road. The woman beside Nina, gliding towards us in colourful, wafting clothes, is her mother. She waves with both arms, quickens her pace, then realises that Nina isn't following on fast enough so she falls back again, laughing. In the past I would have given a wide berth to someone like Natascha. I would have been repelled by her funky appearance and found her brutal honesty irksome. But she's the only person who's not afraid of my grief.

Kaja, who's been leaping about the whole time, prancing on the spot and making little yelping noises, is now unstoppable. She races towards Nina, who continues to sing undeterred. Wagging her tail, Kaja sniffs the girl and won't leave her side for the next hour, while Nina smiles silently. From Natascha I know that Nina takes in everything in her field of vision, but always avoids eye contact.

A strange mother–daughter pair. Whereas the one's life is lived fully outwardly, the other's is turned completely inwards. A nineteen-year-old autistic girl, incontinent, non-verbal, beautiful in an other-worldly way and equipped with a magnificent voice. She knows the way into the house and to her favourite place in the sitting room. The dog accompanies her while I'm enveloped by Natascha's soft arms and the earthy scent of her hair. Omitting the usual niceties, she asks those questions nobody else dares to. "Is the loneliness getting too much for you, Linda?" "Are you still taking sleeping pills?" "What about your husband? How much longer is he going to go along with this?"

Before, in a different life, a life full of possibilities, she studied classical singing. Then came her child and soon the realisation that Nina was different. Her husband left, the possibilities vanished, and mother and child remained in a dark, ground-floor flat that was supposed to have been provisional. Over the next nineteen years Natascha did everything you do for a child you love, but nothing more for herself. Whereas my life only fully opened up when Sonja arrived, Nina's birth was an emergency stop for Natascha.

She beams and points at her bag.

"I've brought cake."

She's wearing bright-red lipstick that makes her mouth look even bigger. Everything about her is a bit too much: too much nose, too bushy eyebrows, too much asymmetry, too much breast and tummy, too much hair, gestures that are too expansive. She teaches voice training at a private music school; I can't think of a better profession for her.

We may not become friends – we're too different for that – but it's the unfamiliarity that enables me to speak more honestly than I can with anyone else. During today's "canine therapy", as we call these hours, I tell Natascha about the other woman.

"What exactly are you expecting from your husband?" she asks.

My answer is hesitant. "For him to have patience."

She laughs and throws her head back. "But he does. He's waited years." Her gaze bores into my eyes. "I think," she says, "you want him to give up like you have. But his life is going on. And you resent him for it."

I don't contradict her.

"You've buried yourself alive here," she adds. When I continue to say nothing, she turns away and joins in the song that Nina is now humming: *Go forth, my heart, and seek delight.*

"Did you know," I say, "that the village used to be a market and people still barter goods here? Eggs and chicken meat in return for repairing a lawn-mower. Or a bucket of sour cherries for a large basket of firewood. Or the ceramicist at the other end of the village – she acquires virtually everything she needs in exchange for her kitsch fruit bowls and colourful vases and cups. If necessary you could survive without money here for a while."

"What's that got to do with your husband, Linda?"

"Nothing. Absolutely nothing."

For a few seconds it's totally silent. Even Nina goes quiet.

"I don't understand how Richard can put it behind him. Could you get over the death of your child?"

"If I'm being honest, I think I could feel happiness again. Not immediately, of course, but over time probably, yes. Nina and I have been through a lot together." Her gaze turns inwards. "A bit too much," she mutters. Then she sighs and looks at me. "Linda! You had seventeen wonderful years with your daughter, you said that yourself. You talked and laughed together, you travelled, you had a happy life for seventeen whole years! Who has that?"

"But I don't have it anymore, either."

"No, you don't. It's something else now."

"But how can he fall in love? How can he feel something like that? I'm utterly incapable of such feelings."

"He's saved himself. On the narrow ridge between life and death he's opted for life, whereas you've tried to pull him over to the dead." She gets up and goes to the wall with the photographs. "You're living with the dead here. Most people in these pictures are no longer alive."

I can't help but laugh. The matter-of-fact way she says this, it doesn't sound terrible in the least.

"How do you actually know he's in love? Maybe he just needs a bit of human intimacy. Some warmth, a caress."

And then she tells me about the man she's sleeping with. He's a fool, but a nice fool. He'd married a woman twenty years younger in the hope of being well catered for sexually, she explains, but after two children the wife's desire was fully spent. Now he comes to visit Natascha every fortnight, sad and starved, and afterwards, grateful and exhausted. He's a good lover. Generous in giving without forgetting how to take. The perfect arrangement, as far as she's concerned.

"What about you? You're too young to live like a nun!"

I'm laughing again. My facial muscles aren't used to this sort of exertion. I can feel each one of them; it's almost painful.

"Pah," I say dismissively, "the desire is no longer there."

Smiling, Natascha rocks her head from side to side and says nothing. Then we eat the cake she's brought – a homemade

Gugelhupf. For Nina, Natascha cuts up a large piece into small mouthfuls and puts the plate on the sofa. Kaja raises her head when Nina puts piece after piece into her mouth without interrupting her singing. We chuckle as she smacks her lips contentedly, and for a while we sit beside each other in silence.

As she's about to go, Natascha tells me she won't be coming past in the next few weeks. For the first time in many years she's having some time off from Nina and her work. She's going on a big trip to the most beautiful Italian islands and, if time permits, a few days in Rome afterwards. Nina is already on her way to the door, Kaja beside her.

"She looks so happy," I say. "At one with herself, in the here and now. And the dog is much calmer with her."

"Nina is the happiest of us all," Natascha says. "In any case, it begs the question of who's providing who with therapy, and why."

With these words she disappears after her daughter, giving me a final wave without turning around.

6

It's Richard's Wednesday, visiting day, but Richard won't be coming. On the phone I asked him not to. I told him I wouldn't know what to say and I didn't want to listen either, especially not to how things were going with "the writer". I couldn't say her name out loud.

He was silent for a while, then said, "If that's what you want."

He seems to have lost his fighting spirit as far as our marriage is concerned.

When Natascha recently pointed out that I was too young for a life without sex, I wondered whether I'd be able to sleep with Richard again. But it remained an anaemic thought. With great effort I managed to picture it in my mind, but the image was lifeless and there was no sensation in my body either. I didn't even feel any resistance. There was nothing, nothing at all.

Richard isn't the last man I slept with. Around fifteen months after Sonja's death I had sex with a complete stranger. Nobody ever found out about it and I never saw him again.

It was the beginning of October and I'd just found out that the reason for the many weeks of difficulty I'd had swallowing, my hoarseness, swollen lymph nodes and night-time sweats, was a papillary carcinoma. My thyroid had to be removed altogether, the doctor explained in his consultation. Then I'd need radioactive iodine treatment to destroy any possible residual tissue. My chances of a full recovery were exceptionally good and I was given an appointment for the operation at reception. Richard, who'd accompanied me to the appointment on a hunch, nodded at everything, asked a whole host of questions, kept reaching for my hand and squeezing it too tightly. As I didn't ask any questions myself, the doctor looked at me occasionally, but basically conducted the conversation with Richard. I saw and heard everything as if from a distance. I didn't feel anything and became impatient. Was there anything we didn't understand, the doctor eventually asked and I said, "No, it's all clear," and went to the door.

Back at reception I was embarrassed at Richard's dogged insistence that the operation must take place in the next few days. The nurse explained kindly and calmly that there weren't any free slots over the coming days and that, not even after twenty years in the job, was she able to pull a surgeon or a free operating theatre out of a hat.

I had thirteen days. Thirteen days under Richard's controlling gaze and his touching but useless morale-boosting chats, which I knew I wouldn't be able to take.

I wanted to be alone. When Richard protested, I replied that this wasn't the time to deny me a simple wish.

I arrived at Rheinsberg station early in the afternoon, went a few kilometres by bus, then walked for around twenty minutes on flagstone and sand paths through a wood. My rucksack was heavy; I'd brought three days' worth of food and drink and intended for this to last me. I followed the instructions that M., a gallerist friend, had sent me, found the key as arranged in a broken bird box beside the terrace of the bungalow, and saw to my surprise that I had mobile coverage.

M. had owned the dacha, which stood empty most of the time, for twenty years, and he'd done barely anything to it in that time. A rampant garden with two old apple trees and a young plum tree surrounded the house. Through a large panorama window you could look out at a small, tranquil lake.

On the first evening I sat on the edge of the jetty that led out into the lake, drinking red wine from the bottle and staring at the dark water. It was cold. The days were still unusually warm, but as soon as the sun went down the temperatures sank rapidly. The chill did me good. As did the drinking. My eyes soon became accustomed to the darkness and, when I saw a light on the other side of the water, my first thought was that it was a car. Then it struck me that the lake was surrounded by woods. According to M. there was no road there, just individual driveways to the few houses and dachas.

When I went back inside the light opposite was still shining. In the dark I pulled a chair up to the window and peered out. From time to time it looked as though the light was moving, coming closer, then moving away again. I found it reassuring not to be completely on my own. In this absolute tranquillity that only exists far from the city, I sat motionless at the window, waiting for the first phone calls. By now Richard would have passed on the news of my cancer to the family. His parents and my mother would get in touch to say the things people say. *We're so sorry . . . What can we do for you . . . You've really had it all, haven't you . . . It never rains but it pours . . .*

My mobile rang. I was still sitting in the dark. I took a deep breath, exhaled, looked at the device vibrating next to me and picked it up. But it was an unknown number. I let it ring until it went to voicemail, which I checked immediately. No new messages.

A sense of unease took hold, making me get up, turn on

all the lights and pace up and down the room. It wasn't long before the phone rang again. It was the same number and this time I answered.

He introduced himself as a friend of M., who'd asked him to help me out if needed. If I had to do some shopping in town or wanted to borrow a bike, if I had problems with the oil radiator, or was afraid of the animals in the woods or just fancied a chat. In short, if I needed anything or was scared, all alone in the remote house . . .

The man spoke these last few words more slowly. He paused, my heart beat faster, pounding like mad, and I looked at the front door. The key was on the inside so I hurried over to lock the door. All of a sudden the panorama window appeared threatening. There was no way of screening it off. Anybody standing outside had a clear view through the window.

He kept talking. Most of the year he lived here beside the lake, he said, and he also looked after M.'s dacha. Had I seen the light on the other side of the lake?

"No," I replied.

I didn't know myself why I lied to him. He responded by saying I should go to the window and look out. Right now he was standing there, he said.

There was silence for a few seconds. All I could hear on the line was static.

"Now you know where you can find me," he finally added.

"Thanks. I'll be fine," I said. "But it's good to know I can call you."

"Any time," he replied.

I hung up, switched the lights off and looked again across the black water at the lit-up house on the other side. How long I sat there, I don't know. The oil radiator was on full blast, now it was hot and sticky in the room, but I didn't dare open a window. At some point the light went off in the other house. All around, shapes and outlines appeared. The night wasn't black, but dark blue, shades of grey, and milky white where the moonlight fell. I spotted the figure at the edge of the property at once. It was moving quickly and nimbly towards the dacha. I turned to look at the door and waited for the knock.

He was barely taller than me, strong, with chiselled features, and I immediately took a dislike to him. Giving me a brazen look, he held up a bottle of wine, said his name and came in. He glanced at the searing oil radiator and grinned. "If you use another two appliances you'll blow the fuse." Then he went over to the window, looked out at his house and said, "I saw you. When I asked you if you'd seen the light on at mine, you said no, but I saw you at the window."

I nodded. I didn't care about having been found out. On the contrary, it set off a chain of events that seemed inevitable and which I didn't have to assume any responsibility for. I was watching a film, looking at a woman and a man from above. I saw him uncork the wine, fill two glasses, the woman drink; I noticed the strained calm of his body, the scar on his right cheek and the barely perceptible twitching of his jaw muscles. A few trivial words were exchanged, a meaningful look from her, then he got up almost abruptly, wished her a good night and left. Slipping back into my body I took up my place at the window again, stared across the lake and waited for the light to go on in the house opposite.

But it remained dark.

When the phone rang I knew it was him.

"Turn off the light, get undressed and lie on the bed," he said.

I did everything he asked and, when I heard his footsteps shortly afterwards, I closed my eyes and let go.

What happened that night belongs in the darkness and silence. Brought into the light and into words it would be incomprehensible.

After he left I slept without sleeping pills, slept more deeply than I had in ages. When I woke up, I stopped being a woman. I spent another two days there before going back to Richard. When he asked how it had been, I said, "Uneventful."

7

The winter lengthens into March, but the days lengthen with it, becoming lighter and luring people out of their houses. They're not unfriendly, the villagers, just economical with their words and chronically mistrustful.

"Been screwed once too often," says my neighbour Klaus.

Soon he brings me a load of wood. Wood's getting dearer, he says this too, just as everything's getting dearer – petrol and gas and electricity and flour and milk and eggs. But I get eggs from my hens and I pay mates' rates for the trailer of wood that Klaus empties in the yard. I'll do the chopping and stacking myself. It'll take days and these days will be bearable. Days with a clear answer to the daily question: Why?

I step outside and am met by an easterly wind. It's been whistling across the fields for days, drying out the top layer of soil and drying me out too. My skin is taut and my hair is charged with static. Thin strands of it stand vertically upwards. I put on my hat, stuffing all the unruly hair beneath it. With Kaja I wander to the rear boundary of the property, from where I look out over the broad fields. Apart from the crows there are still hardly any birds flying across the brown cropland. The no man's land between life and death that I live in is reflected in the landscape, merging with it. Beauty has no business here.

Over at Klaus's the grandchildren are running around the garden. I keep my distance from the fence. They don't live here, the grandchildren; they just come for the odd visit. You don't see any children out and about in the village. There aren't many of them, and for the few that do live here the traffic is too dangerous. Every couple of days or so it claims another victim – a hedgehog, a cat or a raccoon, squashed flat on the road. Sonja would have been horrified; she would have wanted to bury every dead animal. It's something she forced us to do dozens of times. Even individual bits of animals had to be thoroughly interred, like that time we were going for a walk through the dunes between Neuendorf and Vitte on Hiddensee. Sonja ran down to the beach and stopped abruptly. At her feet was a single seagull leg. She kneeled and inspected it, while Richard and I watched a huge, dark-blue cloud empty over the horizon, blurring the line between sky and sea. We were a good quarter of an hour from our accommodation. Richard chivvied the children but Sonja wanted to bury the leg.

"It's your fault if we're hit by lightning," Arvid said impassively. Then he kicked a bit of sand over the gull's leg and said, "There we go, it's buried." But of course this didn't count in my daughter's eyes. Once again I was annoyed by her undue sensitivity. And once again it was Ylvie who responded maternally to Sonja, carefully burying the leg with her in a hollow in the dunes, amongst beach grass. By now the wind was whipping sand into our faces and the dark cloud had become a rapidly advancing black front. I snapped at Sonja, saying something crude, something about the "bloody gull's leg" and how we were all going to get wet now because of the "bloody gull's leg". And of course all of us got soaked to the skin, but by the time we'd run back to the house the sun was peeping out again. We changed into dry clothes and I wanted to tell Sonja I was sorry for my outburst, I really wanted to, but I didn't apologise.

All the things in our lives we leave undone and unsaid, none of these disappear. They accumulate within us, fester and seethe, and sometimes they erupt. On my last visit to the palliative ward, Grete Adomeit, in her agony, was babbling nonsense. It took me a while to realise that she was speaking German and Russian, and so, after almost eighty years since her flight from East Prussia, I became witness to the horrors of those terrible weeks. She flailed about with her arms, called for her mother, muttered Russian commands, moaned and wept. She whispered in a child's voice; I burst into tears and suddenly understood everything that Grete Adomeit had hidden beneath her silence. Those who no longer trust others clutch on to things – a house, a farmyard, a garden. And those who no longer find comfort in others, like me, stand in a garden and keep out of sight of the children on the other side of the fence.

I let Kaja run around and snuffle for another few minutes, then I reverse the car out of the barn and make my way to Leipzig. This is the first time I haven't told Richard I'm coming to the city.

I stop at a florist's, buy some potted pansies, primulas and narcissi and drive on to the white bicycle. All over Leipzig you find these ghost bikes in places where cyclists have been killed in road accidents. Less than two hundred metres from Sonja's memorial bike is another one. The boy was sixteen years old and went to the same school as Sonja. He died two years before she did. Hanging between two trees is a banner with the message: SPEED KILLS.

The traffic whooshes past evenly. Some idiot has tossed their rubbish into the basket of the white bike. From the handlebars hangs a laminated sign with the words SONJA – NEVER FORGOTTEN! and a few photos I'm not familiar with in plastic sleeves. Party pictures of what looks like a drunk Sonja, slightly shocked, glassy eyes, surrounded by three other partygoers I've never seen before. I empty the basket, fill it with the plant pots and put the photos in which my child looks like a drunk into my bag. Sonja rarely touched alcohol. I'm not having anyone remembering her like that.

Back then, a few weeks after her death, I attached the basket to the pannier rack to give everyone who was important to her the opportunity to leave something in it – a photograph, an object, flowers, a letter. The basket filled up quickly, overflowed, and I passed by regularly to make more space. The box with the collection of messages is still in our flat, in Sonja's bedroom. I was obsessed with looking at it all again and again. It was as if it created a connection with Sonja, through which I could be in contact with her for ever. When people eventually stopped putting things in the basket and it remained empty, I began inviting her friends over to listen to their stories about Sonja. Niklas, who she'd recently dated but hadn't slept with; Freya, her best friend since primary school; Lotte, who loved being at ours because her own family consisted only of her and her ever-ailing mother. I invited them in, gave them food and drink, then sucked them dry. I inhaled every word, I drilled them, I probed, not letting go until I'd extracted the last, tiny bit of seemingly irrelevant information about my dead child. For hours I sat with Freya, bent over Sonja's smartphone, the PIN of which I knew. We scrolled through her photos on Instagram and Freya told me who Sonja's followers were. For the most part they were girls of Sonja's age, in the last couple of years at school. Freya told me their names and schools – Hedi from Monte, Lara from Kant, Charlie from EvaSchulze – and explained their connection to Sonja. Sonja's posts, as well as those of the others, felt carefully styled and staged, but harmless and friendly. Fashion, cupcakes, latte art, hair, books, exhibitions, sunsets. No secrets or puzzles were revealed, nothing I didn't know already. I also invited Hedi, Lara and Charlie over, and so every few days there was a young person sitting in our flat, at the mercy of my grief. For I merely acknowledged their own grief, incapable of providing any comfort. In Sonja, Niklas had also lost his first great love. He sat opposite me at our kitchen table a few times with his bristly mullet (Sonja had taught me the English term). With huge headphones around his neck, he answered my questions in monosyllables, and sometimes we just sat there in silence, each of us gazing inwards. Then he'd stagger out and each time the door closed behind him it felt as if my daughter were dying again. On one occasion Richard saw Niklas immediately put his headphones back on by the bike rack outside, light a joint and then, looking dejected, slip away, pushing his bike.

Freya, on the other hand, kept coming back by choice. She needed me as I needed her.

"I can't understand," she often said, "that she's not coming back. I just can't understand it!"

Then she sat on the bed in Sonja's room and stared into space.

I often sat beside her and waited to see if she'd say anything, talk about something I didn't know. And one day I did in fact find out something new.

While Freya talked she kept biting her dry lips. The skin around her mouth was red and inflamed, she licked it a lot and scratched the black polish from her nails, watching the shreds fall onto her jeans.

Without our knowledge Sonja went to see a psychologist about a year before her death. Freya couldn't remember the name of the woman, not even the part of town where her practice was. Sonja went three times. Their first conversation was free; she paid for the next two sessions with pocket money she'd saved. She was desperate to avoid us getting a letter from the health insurance company, which would have given her away. Richard and I mustn't think we'd done something wrong.

"You were such a happy family. Sonja didn't want to ruin this with her problems."

"What do you mean? What problems?"

My question shot out harsher than I'd intended. Freya cowered and shifted slightly away from me.

"You know . . . You were really successful and confident, and Richard so talented. The two of you were such a good couple and Ylvie had these great kids, Arvid was at the art college, and Sonja felt somehow that she wasn't able to match up . . ."

Freya paused and gave me a nervous look.

"You can tell me," I reassured her.

And so I learned that Sonja suffered from anxiety. She was worried about what was going to happen after school, worried about not having a particular talent for anything, having no exceptional skills, worried about not having anything to aim for, about being merely one of many, getting lost in the mass, being overlooked, not shining, glittering, or standing out. She was anxious about getting bad grades, about failure, growing up. She was afraid she wouldn't find a boyfriend, wouldn't have children, wouldn't be loved. And she was worried about disappointing us. Once Freya found her in the loos at school, crying, her heart racing, utterly dejected.

"Panic attacks," Freya said with a shrug. "I get them too. In fact everyone I know does."

In their last session the psychologist advised Sonja to arrange some therapy and she suggested including the family in the process. Sonja rejected this recommendation. Freya remained the only person who knew our daughter didn't want us to have to deal with her pain because we were happy.

I felt dizzy and sick. Leaving Freya in Sonja's bedroom I rushed to the bathroom where I gasped for air and stared into the mirror at the face of the woman who thought she'd known her only child inside out. When I'd recovered slightly and went out into the hall, Freya was already putting her shoes on; the helplessly quizzical look she gave me only baffled me more. As soon as she was out of our flat I dashed back into Sonja's room and started searching. There must be something that would provide some explanation – notebooks, diaries, anything. I pulled the mattress from the bed, turned it over, looked between the slats of the bedframe, emptied her wardrobe and lifted the shelves. But I found nothing. Absolutely nothing.

Richard later found me sitting amongst all that stuff, leaning against the wardrobe, in a state of complete exhaustion. After I'd told him everything, a deep groan rose from his chest. He lifted the mattress back onto the bed and sat down. His lips were as pale as his face when he said, "These days every other person is seeing a psychologist, even if nothing bad has happened. Sonja's anxieties had nothing to do with our family. We live in a society that has produced a totally skewed idea of individualism. Sonja was just normal! But nowadays being normal is treated like an illness. That's all. It's not your fault, Linda."

His conscience was clear, but his words had no effect on me. He couldn't know what I knew. He had no idea how close Sonja had come to the truth.

"It's not our fault," Richard said again, "not yours and not mine."

Freya continued to visit us. For my sake she would rummage around her memories for tiny scraps until one day her parents were at the door, asking me to allow their child to recover and get on with her life.

My next destination is the cemetery. I ignore the many advertising columns at the side of the street, remembering how Sonja, when she was six or seven, would sing a children's song about these columns whenever we passed one; it was verging on a compulsion. I often joined in, which made Sonja laugh and then she'd sing a bit louder. When, eventually, one of the columns pushes its way into my field of vision, I involuntarily mouth the first few words of the song.

I have difficulty breathing. A broken heart isn't just a myth.

In the car park beside the cemetery I wait in the car for a while. My breathing is calmer. I search for the local news station on the radio and listen for a few minutes, with little interest, to what is going on in the world. The world is in turmoil, but nothing of this affects me. Since Sonja's death I've only had this paralysing feeling of total indifference. The distance between me and the world is too great; I hear and read about events, but I don't feel them.

I've become free from fear too, but people get scared of those who have no fear; they're no longer like themselves. Even Esther, my friend who's put up with me the longest without handing out useless advice, and who visited me a few times after my move to the country, became less assured in her dealings with me. Her doggedness had aroused my suspicion. Last time she came, at the end of my first winter in the village, she said, "I get the impression my being here makes you feel worse rather than better."

I didn't contradict her. I remember how good she looked, tanned and muscular after a fortnight on La Palma. She had a new partner – a rich man who'd been prematurely widowed, a "wind-turbine millionaire". Esther went to great pains to avoid appearing too delighted, but there was no mistaking her radiance and I thought her happiness was going to burst out at any moment and soak me.

"If you want me to come, I will," she promised as she left. "Just let me know." At that moment I knew I wouldn't be seeing Esther again for a long time.

I wander past forsythia bushes in bloom, turn into a side street and even from a distance I can see an abundance of colourful flowers billowing from one of the two grave vases and a spring wreath by Sonja's headstone. Has Richard been here? Or Ylvie? She often comes to see her father with her growing bevy of children and usually takes the opportunity to pay a visit to the grave. My own bunch of flowers looks rather wan by comparison. The closer I come, the more my heart pounds. The flowers are very Ylvie but the wreath isn't. Painted clay angels and hearts sit amongst budding sprays of ornamental cherry and white tulips with fringed petals. This arrangement looks touchingly effortful and awkward at the same time. Sonja's friends? Richard's parents? There's no message, no names, just these kitsch angels and hearts.

The thought hits me like a sharp pain. It must have been him. The man responsible for my child's death. The man who knocked her down with his twelve-ton lorry. Thirty-eight years old at the time, married, three children, a lenient judge gave him a ten-month suspended sentence plus three-thousand-euro fine. Involuntary manslaughter, not innocent but unintentional. The man who wept and begged us for forgiveness. The man who will have to live with the consequences of his actions for the rest of his life, just as we have to live with the grief.

We didn't want his money; it went to the national charity for victims of road accidents. Only later did we read that people whose carelessness harmed others counted as victims too. People like him, who I couldn't hate anymore. Who I wanted to kill to begin with, because his death seemed to be the only possible way of settling the score, the only justice. But only until that day when he sat like a heap of misery in the courtroom, ashen-faced, bent and almost as broken as me.

On my way back to the village I stop at the DIY store. I buy mixed seed for the chickens, gladioli bulbs, compost accelerator and a new rake. These days I only buy essentials and things that last. No more clothes, no bric-a-brac.

Kaja is at the gate, waiting for me longingly. I still owe her a morning walk. We head swiftly for the woods and, while she sniffs at scents, I talk to Sonja a bit, tell her about the strange party pictures I found by the bike, admit that I removed them, and also mention the wreath by her grave and the opulent flowers.

"You see? Nobody forgets you," I say out loud.

Then I chat about the dog and tell her how sorry I am that I never let her have a dog, even though it was what she wanted more than anything. "Now I can understand what you were looking for," I say. "It's lovely to have such a loyal friend."

Where the woodland path leads out into open fields I catch sight of the ceramicist from our village. She's crouching on the ground and looks like she's collecting something. Another woman like me, I think, middle-aged, alone with a house, a farmyard and a cat. People say she's slightly crazy. They also say that a younger man comes to visit her. They say quite a few things. As far as my own reputation is concerned I suspect the worst, but that doesn't bother me. I dart a greeting at her as I pass and when we're far enough away I say the word "crazy" a few times in succession. It's crazy, too, how I came to this place, this no man's land whose bleakness now lies before me in its entirety.

Nobody taught me how to deal with fate. I'm a woman without a child, without a husband, without fear and without a future. I hurry back to the farm as fast as I can, bolt the gate and creep back into my lair.

8

Klaus's car and trailer are in the drive, and another load of beech and birch logs are in the middle of the yard. Klaus has unloaded them there and now he's standing beside the pile, nodding contentedly.

"Like it or not, the next winter's bound to come," he says. Then he adds, "It's a lot of work to begin with, but you'll be pleased in the end."

Then he talks about the government's suicidal energy policy, how the political caste has lost touch with the people and how it's driving the country into the ground economically and in other ways. These comments are like bait, but I don't bite. Shaking his head, Klaus says, "Unbelievable." His hand makes a movement like a windscreen wiper across his face and he mutters, "Nutty."

"We don't have time for politics today, Klaus," calls Bruni from the passenger window of his Skoda SUV.

"If it were up to me," he carries on regardless, "all career politicians would need to complete a degree or vocational training and have ten years' work experience on top. That's not asking too much!"

"But it's not up to you!"

His wife's voice again, slightly harsher this time.

I hand him the money for the wood; he puts it in his trouser pocket. A furtive smile brightens his face. "How can you tell a West German from an East German nowadays?"

I shrug.

"The West German trusts his government!"

"Klaus!"

"When the boss calls . . ."

As a parting gesture he touches the flat cap that he wears summer and winter, and gets into the car with his wife.

I've got nothing against these brief conversations with people from the village. They never go deep, never touch the painful points. You come through them unscathed.

The telephone calls with my mother, on the other hand, stick in my head for days. The plaintive tone of her voice hounds me into the nights, forcing me to up my dose of pills. Yesterday evening she said bluntly, "You've got to come to your senses, Linda. Your life isn't over yet." In a somewhat milder tenor, but no less didactically, she added, "You know what Father Ralph says in *The Thorn Birds*. 'For the best is only brought at the cost of great pain.'" *The Thorn Birds* was her favourite book and television series, Father Ralph her great idol.

"What are you trying to say?" I asked. "That my best time is still to come?"

"No, but who knows . . . At any rate, it's not all over and you've got a husband."

I let out a sarcastic laugh which she countered with a brief but intense silence. My grief was also her suffering, she said; my loss weighed down on her soul too. Since Konrad's death (she always said death, not suicide) she hadn't had it easy either, and she couldn't cope with any more bad news. I should go back to Leipzig, back to Richard, before my marriage broke down for good.

"I'm going to hang up now, Mama," I said, and hung up.

I didn't always have the courage to break off a conversation with my mother. The first time I did it was about a year after Sonja died and before my cancer diagnosis. She'd found out from Richard that I was in a bad way, so she called me and, as ever, came straight to the point.

"Linda!" she said strictly. "You've got to force yourself to look to the future now."

She hadn't asked me anything, just thrown in this comment and several other similar ones, studded with lots of *must, bear up, force* and the matching adverbs *onwards* and *upwards.*

In the months after Sonja's death Richard and I were numb with shock, emotionally paralysed, but still capable of doing things despite this inner paralysis. We did everything that was necessary. Everyone was sympathetic. We got offers of help from all quarters and admiration for the lovely funeral, the decorated white bicycle, the beautifully planted grave with the tasteful headstone – marble with a bronze magnolia flower.

It was only when there was nothing more to do, when Sonja's friends stopped visiting us and others began to forget, that the grief hit us with full force. Others' lives went on; our time stood still. We were prisoners of that moment of her death.

April is up to its usual tricks, sending a sudden snow shower. I close the gate, fetch the axe and start splitting the wood. With every stroke I also cut one of my mother's comments in two. I send the axe crashing into her *must* and *force,* into her *onwards* and *upwards.* It's hard work, something that's taken great effort to learn how to do. It requires all my concentration and strength, and the results are a pile of firewood and an appeased me.

Later in the day Gunhild arrives with telescopic loppers and a saw. She lives with her husband Lothar, her daughter, her granddaughter and her ancient mother in the farmhouse opposite. She gives the old apple trees a rejuvenation pruning. Although Frau Adomeit neglected the trees during the last years of her life, they weren't past it, Gunhild reassured me.

"Watch and learn," she instructs me in a friendly tone and I give an obedient nod. I carefully follow her explanations about leaders, lateral shoots and fruit-bearing branches, and already know that I'll forget most of this again.

"Right," she says. "Pay attention!"

She gets onto the ladder, points at a branch and saws it off.

"Competing shoots," she calls out. "They need to go. As well as everything growing downwards or criss-cross – get rid of it."

"Are you a gardener?" I ask.

"Cattle-breeder," she says from up the tree. "Lothar too. There used to be an agricultural cooperative here. Large cattle shed. Half the village worked there."

Now I have to get involved. Gunhild points at a branch and I have to decide if it's to come off or not. Everything thicker than a thumb is sawn, the thinnest branches cut. We work together quickly, exchanging the odd word and keeping our distance. The coffee I offer her afterwards is turned down. She has to get home, she says; her old mother is partial to doing a runner. She's often been brought back by neighbours. Once she fell into the old derelict silo beyond the village. It was a miracle that anyone found her lying on the floor there.

Gunhild sighs, picks up her tools and says goodbye.

I watch as she leaves, striding energetically, her grey, tight ponytail bobbing from side to side. A tall, strong woman I could have happily talked to for longer.

As I gather up the prunings and load them into the wheelbarrow, my phone vibrates in my trouser pocket. Richard has sent a short message and a picture of the magnolia outside our block. It's in full, magnificent blossom in a flurry of snow. My heart cramps. Sonja loved that tree; when the wind blew off the petals she'd stand beneath it and let them land on her.

I don't answer him, but push the wheelbarrow with the prunings to the very rear of the property where the fence is broken and I've built a wall of dead wood. Klaus helped me knock in a few posts, and now I pile all the larger branches and twigs there.

Another message from Richard. *When are we going to see each other?*

I'm not going to be able to keep him away any longer. Since his Brida confession we've messaged each other a few times but haven't met up. Something's bothering him. I can sense it from his tentative language, his cautious tiptoeing around the kernel of a truth that he doesn't want to put into words. After so many years together we need to look each other in the eye when discussing something important.

The new significant thing in his life has an unusual first name, which I've already searched online. When I added "Leipzig" and "writer" I got more than 500,000 hits. She looked different in every image. Sometimes laughing and very attractive, in some pictures her head back, a superior air on her face, sometimes clever, serious and tired, then with a cheeky smile like a little girl. Sometimes her hair is up, sometimes down, blonde, then red. She wears heels, skirts and blouses as confidently as she does trainers with jeans and a sweater. She's written literary novels, short stories, a novella and several crime novels. The crime novels made it onto the bestseller lists and she decided to stick with this more successful formula. She's given a few interviews on subjects such as hunting, animal protection and vegetarianism. As the daughter of a forestry worker and in possession of a hunting licence herself, she argues coolly and objectively, explains how useful hunting is for preserving habitats and the balance between species, and advocates for an understanding of nature that goes beyond the romantic ideas of city dwellers. In this country, nature is no longer a space that human beings have to leave alone, she insists; people are part of this space and their intervention is necessary in a controlled way. She hasn't given her opinion on bigger social topics, or at least I couldn't find any. Her previous partner, on the other hand, the lawyer and lecturer Hans-Peter Mehrlich, has a long list of publications on the controversial issues of our times. Wikipedia labels him a conservative, but what does that mean? The titles of his articles are: "Enough now!", "Act according to the reality principle", "Against the ideological impetus". Wikipedia also reveals the years when the relationship between Brida Lichtblau and Hans-Peter Mehrlich began and ended, from which I deduce that he isn't the father of her children. He's not dissimilar to Richard – tall, slim, almost lanky, slightly asymmetrical facial features, glasses, grey hair.

They'll look good together, Brida Lichtblau and my husband.

Jealousy is good for me. It burns like a small fire in my chest, warming my stomach, colouring my cheeks red. But while I layer the prunings on my wall of wood, pressing them down firmly, I'm struck by the realisation that I won't fight to keep him.

When are we going to see each other? Richard wrote.

Whenever you like, I reply.

*

In bed that evening I push a pill from the blister pack and place it on the bedside table. You can take it any time, I tell myself. It's there, nobody's going to pinch it. Then I close my eyes and begin my descent towards sleep. But shortly before landing, shortly before the distinct structures of consciousness begin to disintegrate, I rise up again. My heart is racing and I can clearly hear my mother's voice. She's issuing warnings, threats and prophesies of doom and gloom. I put my hands over my ears but it's no use. All her words trickle into me again, dripping word by word into my mind. "Don't put your marriage on the line. Come to your senses. Go back to your husband. That isn't your life out there."

She doesn't mean me, I think; she means the other Linda – the old Linda.

The old Linda wouldn't have known how to deal with the villagers here. The old Linda surrounded herself with people who knew about contemporary art and literature, and who got lost in thought spirals, at the end of which there was no longer anything absolute. The friends of old Linda wore sneakers with expensive linen dresses or casual suits, rode racers and had handbags made out of old Tetra Paks. They invested their money in ethical ETFs, making tidy profits, and as soon as they had children they would rent an allotment where they would install a Swedish-style wooden cabin – white with blue window frames and a small veranda at the front. There they would grow vegetables in raised beds and buy an electric cargo bike to transport compost, plants and organic things for the barbecue to the garden, and children to their toddler music lessons. They let their older children, who they maintained friendly relationships with, lecture them about flight shame and make them promise only to travel by train from now on and to buy at least half their groceries in a zero-waste shop. These parents did everything for their children and were rewarded with comments like, "It's really nice the way my parents support me." So as far as the old Linda is concerned, my mother is spot on. But she knows nothing about the new Linda.

I calm myself down, reach for the pill just to feel it, inhale for four seconds and exhale for eight. After the tenth cycle my heart is beating serenely and evenly, and I sink into sleep.

But once again, like a pilot who's failed to make the landing strip, I thrust upwards, high up into the icy cold air of my wide-awake consciousness. And my mother is still on board. Undeterred, she says, "Come to your senses. Don't put your marriage on the line. Go back to your husband." Ludicrous comments from *her* mouth.

"Richard was never good enough for you," I say out loud and remind her that Konrad and she didn't approve of him until he "finally saw reason".

Painting pictures that nobody's waiting for – Richard stuck this out for a long time, almost two decades. He'd seen his former fellow students become well-known names, had gone to their exhibitions and congratulated them on their global success as representatives of the New Leipzig School, whereas his own store of pictures filled up without the world taking notice. When schools began to employ people from other sectors to combat the universal teacher shortage, he'd been working at his friend Hauke's shop for around fifteen years. Richard had a university degree, and after three months of introductory training he was given a fixed-term contract as an art teacher at a Leipzig secondary school. Only then did he meet with my parents' approval.

The realm of sleep is now far below me. I place the index and middle fingers of my right hand on my carotid artery and count seventy-eight beats per minute. I take the pill from the bedside table and push another out of the blister pack, swallow both and wait to sink. My limbs grow heavy and my mother's voice recedes. I can still hear it, but the white mist of sleep, which is getting ever thicker and enveloping me, removes the voice's sharpness and it fades into the background. Finally I land.

I'm awake just before four. My pulse is high and I'm gasping for air. At the open window I breathe the panic away as one of the DHL freight planes drones across the village. My mother's voice is back too. I thought I was rid of it, thought it had been smothered by sleep. "Don't put your marriage on the line," it says, just like yesterday evening, as if it had never gone away. But now I remember another remark from the lips of the same woman, but many years earlier: "What are you doing with this man?"

At home in Kronberg "this man" remained a foreign body. His lack of interest in the trappings of the external world, in possession and wealth, securities, cars and property, prevented a flowing conversation with my stepfather, who simply didn't know what to make of "this man". For Richard made no effort to hide how little interest he had in the great potential of new stock from the raw materials sector, which according to Konrad ought to be part of every portfolio. He didn't feign admiration when Konrad spoke about the expensive Hurtigruten cruise to the Antarctic that he was planning with my mother.

"What are you doing with this man?"

The question didn't miss its mark. For "this man" didn't match the idea of him that I'd bravely presented to my mother. As soon as we entered the house in Kronberg and Konrad embraced me, my gaze shifted to Richard. I was looking for the doer in him, but only saw the loser. I was looking for the man who would move forwards, clear all obstacles out of the way, the protector and of course the breadwinner. And because I couldn't find what I was looking for, incomprehensible words poured from my lips the moment we were alone in my old room. Those who don't think big have a fear of failure. Those who limit their ambitions to a minimum show they have a narrow-minded world-view. It was nothing but a cheap trick to avoid disappointment. Richard called it my "Kronberg illness". Only once did he retort, with unusual severity, that I was free to leave at any time and look for a younger, loaded version of my stepfather, anaesthetised by permanent consumption. From then on he dismissed my outbreaks like an allergic sneeze.

Now, in the cold morning air, my mother's voice falls silent. It was a long road from "What are you doing with this man?" to "Don't put your marriage on the line!" The comments are separated by two deaths.

My stepfather Konrad died a good year before Sonja. While my mother and a friend of hers were floating in the warm water of a rooftop pool at a wellness hotel, Konrad drove his car into the garage of their house in Kronberg, closed the door, fixed a hose to the exhaust and put the other end inside the car. He put the window up enough so that the hose was wedged but not clamped, sealed the rest of the opening with cling film and sticky tape, put a large stone on the accelerator and listened to Schubert's *Winterreise*. His heart must have been racing by "Gefror'ne Tränen", maybe he was already unconscious by "Lindenbaum" and died to "Rückblick". He can't have made it to "Täuschung" or "Der Wegweiser". Konrad loved the *Winterreise*. He owned almost every recording. Deep down he was a romantic.

The official reason for his suicide that my mother told her circle of friends was the Parkinson's diagnosis he'd received shortly before. What she kept quiet about was the disastrous speculation in which Konrad had gambled away most of their fortune. Only my brother and I found out about this.

Richard's grief was kept to a minimum. He found it absurd that someone should kill themselves over lost money, ludicrous even. Surprisingly, Sonja didn't agree, and said something that's stuck in my mind ever since: "I can understand wanting to disappear if you've disappointed everyone."

9

The pictures are like magnets.

They don't give us the choice; they draw us up from our chairs, through the door into the sitting room and to the wall, where Richard and I are now standing again. First I look at Grete Adomeit's relatives, the still, serious faces of her parents and siblings in one of their last summers in the East Prussian homeland, before the catastrophe that destroyed everything, which, bizarrely, is already written on their faces. Then I look at our old life, at the happiness, the prosperity, the peace and lack of worries, and think: I had it all, experienced everything, did my duty. This part is over. From now on everything is optional.

I gaze into Sonja's sparkling eyes, which radiate an innocence that must have been a result of our protectiveness. I recall a conversation with Richard about this very subject – Sonja's naivety and her assumption that everyone was intrinsically good.

"Do you remember when we were worried about her because she was so kind-hearted?" I say.

He nods. "You were more worried than I was."

"Yes," I reply. "I was always more worried than you. I had more to lose."

At the local kindergarten and primary school, Sonja found friends whose parents were just as protective of their children as we were. Insulated from the iniquitous demands of an aesthetically and morally suspect environment, they grew up in that typical middle-class bubble which I hoped would envelop Sonja her whole life long. I couldn't bring myself to sow suspicion, mistrust or fear in her pure heart; I was successful in avoiding it, and that was why I worried about her. I always needed to know where she was, when she was coming home, who she was meeting. She always had to leave her phone switched on and she never protested against this.

"It's fine, Mama, it's perfectly natural that you want to know where your daughter is," she would say sympathetically each time I enquired, for no reason at all, where she was and what she was doing.

I'll be ten minutes late, she would message me at five to ten when she was supposed to be home at ten and wasn't going to make it in time. In the hall was a list of phone numbers of her friends and their parents, and the families of Freya, Lotte and a few others had our number too.

Richard thought I was intrusive. When he was seventeen he'd have rebelled against a mother like me.

"When we were seventeen we were pretty much grown-ups," I said.

But Sonja wasn't a grown-up. She died before she could become one.

The two of us are now looking at the same photo, the last one before her death. She's laughing and looking candidly at the camera; I wonder if what I'm seeing is real.

"I hope that in the last moment of her life she didn't realise it was her last moment," I say to Richard. I can see a touch of irritation in his face.

"We could take a trip," he says out of nowhere.

"A trip? What sort of trip?"

"Anywhere, doesn't matter. I want to find out what's left of us."

"What's happened to Brida?" I ask. "Aren't you seeing each other anymore?"

"Yes, we are. It's nice with her . . . but hard work too."

"Hard work?"

"She's . . . she's intense."

I don't pursue the matter. I've found videos of her, clips from readings, interviews. She's a bundle of energy. A never-say-die woman with high body tension. Someone who sucks others dry because she constantly wants something. In five years' time he's going to be sixty. Has she thought about this?

"I can't start anything new without having finished what came before," he says. "Are we really at the end, Linda?"

I say nothing.

He excuses himself and goes to the bathroom. At the door he turns around. "I want an answer to my question."

When he comes back his hands are full of boxes of pills. He drops them all onto the sitting-room floor, then picks them up again, one by one, and reads out the names of the drugs: Lunivia, Mirtazapine, Zopiclone, Doxepin, Temesta, Zolpidem, Quetiapine, Amitriptyline, Tavor.

"Do you take all of these?" he says, looking at me in disbelief.

I explain that I change the combination of the medicines, but never take more than two at any one time. Lunivia plus Quetiapine, for example, or Zopiclone plus Mirtazapine. Sometimes, on bad evenings, I'll have two Zopiclone plus a Quetiapine or a Tavor.

"How can I know you're not going to swallow them all at once?" he says.

"You can't," I say.

"For Christ's sake, Linda. This is a shitshow!"

"It's not that easy to kill yourself with pills," I reassure him. "The chance of surviving with permanent damage is high. And you have to take Vomex beforehand, otherwise you throw the whole lot up again. Have you seen a pack of Vomex anywhere?"

"No Vomex! Well, that *is* reassuring," he says with audible cynicism.

He's so worn out and annoyed that he's going to turn his back on me soon. I know it. I'd do exactly the same. Nobody's patience is infinite.

I pile the boxes of pills on top of each other and return the tower to the bathroom. "Come on," I call out as cheerfully as possible, then chuck Richard his coat and take Kaja by the lead.

The woods are at their most beautiful at this time of year – the ground covered with green and all the dainty, early flowering plants that defy the night-time frosts. Birds are clearly visible in the open crowns of the trees. Later in the year I'll only be able to hear them and guess at where they're hiding in the thick foliage. Now the sun reaches the forest floor almost unhindered.

Richard takes off his cap and stuffs it in his coat pocket. He doesn't want to leave without having got an answer from me. I could promise him that I'll come back. I could suggest something – a new us, a future as a couple, a place we'd live together. It would be easy because he's waiting for something like this and wouldn't ask questions. I can see it in his dark, tired eyes, that are saying nothing about a new beginning with another woman. Basically I don't envy Brida.

He keeps looking at me in expectation. We walk slowly and to him my silence must seem loud. I've got to say something.

So I tell him about the abyss I keep gazing into and which draws me in. There are numerous triggers. Sometimes it's my mobile phone, spontaneously showing me photos, flashbacks to three, five or seven years ago. All of a sudden Sonja will appear on the screen, hanging upside down from a climbing frame; thickly wrapped up with a rucksack, arm in arm with her best friend Freya, as the school ski trip was about to leave for Austria; or one of our silly selfies. More often it's smells. The faint aroma of Christmas biscuits from an open window tears me away from one second to the next. For a while I believed that every fit I had would make the next one more bearable. I hoped that if I gave myself up to my grief without resistance, I would soften it or even use it up like a bottle of bitter medicine. But I was wrong. When grief comes it comes with a consistent force.

"I don't know how I can live, how I can still be here when Sonja isn't. I really don't," I say to Richard.

"But you are living! You get up every day and do your chores around the place."

"I'm not a burden to anyone here. I live from hour to hour, survive one day at a time. It's no more than that, nor does it have to be out here. Nobody's expecting anything from me. With you it would be different." When he doesn't respond I say, "You see? I'm right."

It's become warm. We take off our coats and sit on the trunk of a fallen tree.

"My mother's turning eighty next week." Richard looks at me thoughtfully. "She'd like you to be there. Who knows how many more birthdays she'll have." Taking my hand he rubs his fingers gently along it. "It's important to me."

I picture the celebration, my parents-in-law Ingrid and Hans, Ylvie with her beautiful children, Arvid, and Richard's self-assured sister with her husband and children. All of them will stare at me, scrutinise, silently evaluate my healing process, treating me with consideration but like a patient, someone who's expected to make more of an effort, get involved a bit more.

People tire of other people's suffering. They lose the inclination to be considerate, want to be able to complain again themselves. Secretly they're furious that every one of their own problems pales in comparison to mine. My presence forces them to realise how lucky they are. I know this because I was like that too. So impatient and unwilling to acknowledge fate.

"I'll think about it," I say to Richard.

I'd like to lean my head on his shoulder, rest it there for a moment. As if he's sensed this urge he puts an arm around my shoulder and pulls me towards him. I still enjoy smelling him. It's the scent of a familiar intimacy and happy years, the scent of the past. It almost feels unreal that something of Richard has remained undisturbed by Sonja's death, that his smell has been salvaged to still exist in the present. I breathe him in like a longing, a dream.

When we reach the village Klaus comes over to us.

"Have a nice walk? Any more plans for today?"

We shake our heads and realise at once that this question was just a pretext. In the past, Klaus tells us, they used to have everything here, even dancing on Saturday evenings. From seven to eleven there was a disco in the function room of the Roter Stern. Sometimes a decent band would play too. Young people came from all the neighbouring villages, had an enjoyable evening and still got up the next day. It's all different now, he tells us. Now they don't set off until eleven, going to clubs in Leipzig. But the human body hasn't changed. It sleeps at night and is awake during the day. To make it through these nights and keep going till the following morning they down energy drinks and take drugs and heaven knows what else. No, it's not right at all, but what can you do?

Then he wishes us a nice evening and goes on his way.

Richard grins. "Everything used to be better," he says, imitating Klaus, and looking at me in the hope that I'll agree. At the gate I say goodbye to him – without any regrets. I want to be alone now. Richard emphasises once more how important it is for him that I come to Ingrid's birthday, then he gets into the car, gives a brief hoot, waves and drives off.

10

I'm able to read again.

After Sonja's death it was impossible. I couldn't concentrate on anything for more than ten minutes, and every piece of writing produced images that tried obsessively to connect with my daughter's life. Until recently there were only four books in this house: a guide to birds, one on dog training and two gardening books.

On my kitchen table there is a bunch of tulips in a glass vase, in front of them the book. I bought it today, even though the woman in the shop warned me about the contents. It's a sad book, she said. Not one for dark days. A Norwegian writer, a story about two girls, one of whom disappears.

The tulips in the vase are an intense dark reddish orange with yellow fringes. Closed, the flowers look like carnivorous plants. Sticking a finger into one of the half-open ones, I'm surprised when nothing happens.

I've overheated the kitchen so I take off my woollen jumper. It's been raining and stormy since yesterday evening. Kaja is lying languidly at my feet, making the occasional human-sounding noise. I open the first page. "A young, white forehead boring through the darkness." I'm drawn in at once.

It takes a message from Richard to haul me back to reality.

A group photo of his family, his mother in the middle with a bunch of flowers, beneath it the words: *You were missed.*

Another message follows: *Shame . . . It's still all about you, never anyone else.*

Ingrid turned eighty without me being there. While she was entertaining her guests I was planting herbs in an old ceramic sink that someone had left in front of their house for taking. While she was on her traditional stroll through Dresden with her guests, with an excursion to Goethe's house, I planted gladioli bulbs in various spots in the garden.

It's still all about you, Richard writes today, *never anyone else.*

I refrain from explaining to him the gulf between *not wanting to* and *not being able to*. If I'd had the strength I would have gone and fulfilled my daughter-in-law duty. But yesterday morning I wasn't even able to get up from the breakfast table. I sat there as if glued to my chair, my feet getting ever colder and my limbs stiffening. Kaja howled a lament, scratched at the door, eager to go out, but I just sat there and couldn't stand up.

By lunchtime I'd managed to get dressed and brush my teeth. After that I slept for an hour and waking up was anything but fun. I know when it's worth fighting and when not; I know what I have left. You can't get anything out of an empty tank.

I can't understand why he's so angry. I mean, I'm doing what I can.

I didn't realise how dependent I am on his understanding. He's the only one who's lost her too, the only one whose feelings mirror mine, and his intelligent heart usually gifts him the right words. When I got cancer and saw it as permission to give up, he said, "I can't lose you too." When I had no answer to this, he added a comment that I still carry around with me: "If your life only had a point when you were happy, then it never had a point."

Before Sonja I was a person with autonomous feelings, but incomplete, an individual without a context. When she was born my happiness was subjugated to hers. From the very start of her life all the way to beyond her death, I have been what she is – happy, unhappy, anxious, sad, euphoric, alive or dead. For when a child goes, they take you with them. They leave you as no more than a shrivelled husk.

Has it been like this for mothers in all eras? Did the sheer number of children help? Was it easier to let one of six go because five remained? Were hearts harder and the will to live stronger? In the past it used to be a misfortune if a family had only one child, whereas these days it's a decision. With just a single child your freedom is still considerable; with none it's limitless. But without attachment, freedom is worthless.

We mothers of one child are strange beings. We place all our expectations and love in this one offspring. We're bold gamblers, too, putting everything on one card. And then: *rien ne va plus.*

I've lost the game.

Richard's voice in my head says, "If your life only had a point when you were happy, then it never had a point."

I call his number. I want to hear the voice of the man who believes there's also a point to my life when I'm suffering, and who's now levelling the accusation that it's only about me.

"Hello, Richard," I say.

"Hello, Linda," he says, then describes the park bench where he's spending his lunch break before having to teach more lessons.

"I think I'm going to get sunburned," he says. "My skin isn't used to the sun yet."

"Why are you angry at me," I ask.

"I'm not angry. I'm sad, disappointed. Everyone's asking after you and I don't know what to tell them anymore."

"Tell them the truth, Richard. Tell them I'm broken. Tell them about Brida."

All I can hear is his breathing.

"What about you?" he says. "Are you in the sun too? It's almost like summer today."

"No," I say, my gaze sweeping the dark room. I've lost the craving for summer. My inner winter can't be attuned to the levity of the bright, warm days.

"Go outside," Richard says. "You have to live, despite everything."

"I will," I say.

He wants to know if there's anything I'm missing out here.

"I'm missing Elvana," I say, and at once I see her vividly with her dyed red hair and curvy backside in tight leggings. She cleaned for us once a week. We didn't always see each other – she had her own key – but whenever we did she made me laugh. Once, when Richard spent three months at an artists' retreat in the Wendland, she thought he'd left me.

"I been thinking," she said slyly, "and I think you need new husband. Wife without husband not good. Like pot without lid. I found good man for you. My brother. Is good man. Not run away."

When I mentioned this to Richard he burst out laughing.

Or the time I was in bed with flu. She peered around the door and whispered quite loudly, "I have tip from doctor in Kosovo. You must take lamp oil with sugar. Twelve days then better. Lamp oil, Linda. Make cancer go and everything."

She was younger than me, but she hardly had any of her own teeth left. When her dentures hurt she would put them on a plate in the kitchen then give a hearty laugh.

"Elvana. So you're missing nothing apart from her," Richard says matter-of-factly.

"What do you want me to say, Richard?"

He gives a bitter laugh. "It's not about what I want to hear. It's about what you're not feeling."

"That's a complicated subject. On the phone I can't—"

"You were the one who rang me, Linda."

"Yes, I know," I say. After a pause, I add, "Could you come over?"

He sighs, then says, "Can't you come here? I finish at 3.45."

For a while I sit at the kitchen table, twiddling the car key in my fingers. I get up, go to the bathroom and look in the mirror. I wash my face and brush my hair. First one way, then the other, then back again, harder and harder until my scalp is glowing. I run through the journey in my mind, thinking about how to avoid the busy roads, where I can park, how long I'll need. I'm finding thinking difficult. As if the information has to overcome a blockade. As if passage along the neural network is being hindered by an obstacle, the grief barrier. Everything needs to find its way over this.

I put down the brush and message Richard that I'm not going to make it. *Dear Richard, I don't feel up to coming,* I write.

He arrives shortly after five o'clock. He comes in, puts his arms around me and holds me tight.

We go out into the yard and sit in the sun. His silence is so calming that I close my eyes. I sense the sun going down, losing its power of warmth, and the longer we sit there the more impossible I find it to break the silence. The traffic roars incessantly on the main road. Now, late in the afternoon, it's an even noise like a waterfall.

Richard gets up abruptly. He takes a few steps then turns to me and says, "I can't do this anymore, Linda. I know I shouldn't be putting you under pressure, but I'm just a misery guts next to you, and I can't go on like this."

I look at him. The words are locked up inside me.

He says I've got to stop running away. I should realise that we need each other, that we belong together more than ever. He's blocking out the sun, but it's going to disappear behind a house soon anyway.

"There's one thing I've been meaning to ask you for some time," he says. "Were you happy with us, before Sonja died? If you had really been happy we wouldn't be at this point now. We'd get through this together."

I think about it, trying to remember the Before, my feelings, but Richard suddenly shakes his head.

"There's no point anymore, Linda. You're not giving me anything I can hold on to."

"I'm sorry," I say.

Our goodbyes are different from usual. The hope is shattered. Richard's patience is exhausted. I can see it in his eyes and yet I let him go.

I'm staying here. Here I can't do any damage. The black hole inside me isn't pulling anyone into the abyss. I should never have been allowed to have a child, I think. I'm too feeble for such a love.

11

Natascha's back from her holiday. She's sitting beside me on the bench in the yard. Her shoes are off and she does a sort of foot gymnastics while we chat. Her toenails are multicoloured.

She's brought me presents: a turquoise bracelet and an olive-wood rosary made – and allegedly blessed – by the monks at a monastery. I put on the bracelet.

"The stones look amazing against brown skin," Natascha says, making me aware that I've got some catching up to do on this front.

I don't really know what to do with the rosary; I let it slide through my fingers, wondering about the T-shaped cross. Natascha tells me that the tau cross is the symbol of the Franciscans.

"Don't think about it, just hang it up somewhere," she says.

Meanwhile Nina and Kaja can't keep still. Nina turns around and around, waving her thin arms as if they were wings and singing the Queen of the Night aria with such purity of tone.

Natascha rolls her eyes. "When she sings that, she's had enough. She wants to go."

Kaja trots patiently beside Nina until the girl calms down, the voice becomes softer and the melody changes to a folk song that sounds familiar. Nina sits on the ground a safe distance from us and Kaja immediately lies next to her.

"See?" Natascha says, audibly breathing in and out. The holiday tan is peeling from her arms, she's put her hair up into a sort of nest, and the energy coming off her seems dense, almost tangible. I shift away from her slightly.

"You need to get away from here too, Linda," Natascha says, making it sound like an order. She rummages for her phone and slides back up close to show me pictures from her trip. She was on Ischia and Sardinia, where she met people, locals, got photographed with them, in front of their shops, flower beds and in picturesque old streets. I want to ask her how she does that, meet new people, but she swipes from one photo to the next. Most of them are typical selfies: her with a beaming smile.

"You look happy," I say.

She glances at Nina and her face turns dark. "Pictures lie. You know that. But yes, there were some happy moments. Only, Nina was in a bad way. She always ends up paying for it."

She puts the phone away and sighs.

"Nina was ill. Nothing serious, just a bad cold, but she wasn't well looked after. No cream for her sore nose, no nasal spray. With her blocked nose she barely slept. Her lips were so dry, they were chapped all over, she lost weight, got eczema in the nappy area, hands bitten sore, open wounds on her legs from scratching, plaque on the teeth, hair loss. And all of this while I was having a good time in Italy."

"That's dreadful," I say. "But you need a break too."

"I can't enjoy a break if it means my daughter's going to the dogs."

At that moment Nina begins to laugh. Kaja lifts her head, pricks up her ears and Nina laughs even louder. Then we laugh too. We laugh until the tears come and my facial muscles ache.

"So long as we can still laugh not everything's lost," Natascha says when we've composed ourselves. "Am I right, Linda?"

"Probably."

"If you had one wish, Linda, a realistic one, nothing impossible . . ."

She removes the pencil from her nest of hair and runs her fingers through the mane as it tumbles down. I shrug.

"Anything, it doesn't have to be special."

I want my daughter back, I think, and say, "I don't have a wish."

"Hmm . . . OK . . . Well, if one does come to mind then say it out loud, in the present tense, as if it were already coming true. Never in the conditional, Linda, that's important."

I can't help bursting into laughter for the second time today.

"Yes, really!" she says. "You have to try it. Sometimes it works."

Nina suddenly leaps to her feet and scampers to the gate on her thin legs. Natascha sighs and follows her daughter.

For a while I watch them go, this strange, singing mother–daughter team. Next door the gate opens and Klaus comes out into the street. Putting his hands on his hips he looks in the same direction.

"I mean . . . the girl's a mess," he states. Then he proceeds to tell me who else in the village is a mess. Christian Kühn is a mess because of booze, Thomas Haffner because of his nasty wife, the Schmidts' son because he contracted meningitis when he was a child, and Gunhild and Lothar's daughter because of recreational drugs. A host of messed-up people.

"What about me?" I ask.

"You?" He stares at me, wide-eyed, as if he doesn't know what I mean. Then he nods a few times and eventually says, "*You* need to watch out. Anyone who lives on their own for too long becomes weird. Cranky. And then—"

"And then I'll be a mess," I say, finishing his sentence.

"Possibly," he says, tapping his peaked cap as a goodbye before crossing the road on bandy legs.

I close the gate, fetch hammer and a nail from my toolbox, knock the nail in above the entrance to the chicken shed and hang the rosary from it. Let the chickens be protected, I think; I've no use for it myself. Nothing that happens to me can be worse that what I've already been through.

Kaja is lying in the shade of a lilac bush, yawning.

"If I end up a mess you'll have to find another mistress," I tell her. "Try Bruni and Klaus first," I say, but there's no reaction except a twitch of her left ear.

Natascha has left a flyer on the kitchen table – her choir is singing in St Peter's in Leipzig, but I'm not going to go. I can't risk bumping into old friends. I don't want to watch them try too hard, avoiding saying anything about their children so as not to hurt me. I can't stand it when they talk about their children either. I can't cope with their uncertainty or their attempts to be helpful, and least of all their looks of concern. And I know what they're thinking: Thank God it wasn't my child! They try to empathise with the suffering of the orphaned mother, have a brief dabble with the emotional upset, but with the comforting feeling of being one of those who's been assigned a kinder fate.

We live in separate worlds now. A glass wall stands between us and I'm not going to break it.

12

Shoots have appeared from all the gladioli bulbs. I planted seventeen, and seventeen young plants have broken their way through the surface of the soil and are craning towards the sun.

Richard is craning towards the sun too. He and Brida are now officially a couple.

"I've got to give it a go," he said, adding, "You left me with no choice."

He'd come out specially to tell me this, justifying his decision with the best arguments and promising still to be there for me in the future, just not quite so regularly and of course no longer as my husband.

"As what, then?"

"Your friend, a close friend." He looked as if he had bitten into a grapefruit.

"We're still married," I replied in the sober tone of a statement.

"Nothing need change in that respect, Linda."

He made a movement as if to give me a hug, but then stopped.

I asked to see a photo of Brida even though I'd googled her dozens of times.

Richard hesitated, but then took out his phone, swiped the screen for a while and gave it to me. In his face I saw a faint pride and something in his bearing changed. He was radiating a hint of healthy masculinity.

"A beautiful woman," I said, but that was beside the point. Her eyes were sparkling, her smile was genuine, her face relaxed. I made no effort to hide my feelings. It wasn't jealousy or grief or anger making my hands shake and lips quiver, but envy at her capacity for pleasure. There was no glass wall between her and the world. There would never be a photo like that of me again.

Richard carefully took the phone off me and put it away. "You can't force your hermitic lifestyle on me for ever."

I gave no response to this apart from a nod. He was right. His interest in life had been reawakened a while ago. He painted almost every free afternoon and at weekends, and even his feelings of lust had returned. Without sex, he explained, he was dead artistically too. There was a direct correlation between the vitality of his work and the vitality of his body, My "hermitic lifestyle" stood in the way of his recovery.

When he said goodbye I let him give me a lengthy hug and as he drove off I could still feel his hands on my back.

My fingers run over the firm tips of the gladioli leaves. It's May. There's no holding nature back. Everything is surging with life. Plump buds are bursting open, the peony flowers are exploding and the garden is screaming growth and renewal, flaunting vibrant colours. In the village the gates open, people are friendlier with their greetings, they're looking for conversation and, in the evenings, the aromas of barbecues and children's laughter drift over the fences and hedges. At no other time of the year is the world around me in such stark contrast to how I feel. In winter, when the inner and outer grey coalesce, coming together in unison, I can breathe more easily.

Now I struggle through the jollity of these days as through a bad storm, and the only comfort is the unfailing end. Only when the hot, dry summer days scorch the green, dry up the shallow water, every living thing is groaning from the aridity, and finally the autumn wind tugs at the prematurely withered leaves, will I be released from the burden of enforced cheer.

I cocoon myself, switch off my phone, draw the curtains of the windows facing the road and bolt the door. Alone with Kaja, the chickens, the dead people on the wall and the living memories, day after day passes.

I exist.

I wish something would deliver me. Something devastatingly beautiful, a force of nature – a conflagration, a storm tide, whirlpool. But nothing happens. There's only the wind sweeping across the dry countryside, creeping up on the farmyard, surmounting gates and roofs, blowing up the dust.

I breathe and vegetate. I eat only once a day. For a week I haven't spoken to anyone except my animals and Sonja. Once a day I switch on the phone, give those who are worried about me a sign of life, then turn it off again. With every day that passes my fear of a real encounter grows.

The wind unsettles me. It gives me headaches. The chickens too seem more nervy than usual. The moment I open the door to the shed they come storming out, clucking wildly, running, flapping and making a racket. They don't start scratching and pecking until the cockerel intervenes. Today I've peeled carrots and diced apples. The cock and his favourite hens fill their bellies before taking a dust bath in the sandpit. The other hens copy them afterwards. I planted mint, rhubarb and a wild rose, in an attempt to prettify their run, but there isn't much left of them. The hens eat more quickly than the plants grow. The big rhubarb leaves were going to provide shelter from the rain and sun, or at least that's what I'd imagined. Klaus's curt solution was: "Wire-netting fence." I've learned everything I know about hens from him. When the flock cleans their plumage all together, that's a sign of a stable pecking order, he says. Apparently hens cackle after laying an egg and sometimes cockerels praise them by starting to cackle too.

I watch the birds for a while, amazed by their curiosity, their permanent busyness, their individuality. Amongst the hens there are daring and shy ones, flirtatious, cheeky and unassuming ones. The most inquisitive of the lot is Pippilotta. I gave her this name after she survived the buzzard attack. When Kaja accompanies me into the chicken enclosure and lies down, Pippilotta often comes scuttling out and hops onto her back. I used to see chickens as food. Now I sit amongst them and I know I won't eat a single one.

Every evening I abandon myself to the flood of memories. With each image comes pain. It strikes my body like lightning, boring into my heart, into my brain and my guts, leaving me gasping for air and turning my legs to jelly. When it subsides, this comes not as a relief but a paralysis from exhaustion which, in the best-case scenario, leads to a leaden semi-sleep.

It was like this back then too, a few months after Sonja's death, when the days and nights merged sluggishly and suddenly I was able to see it: almost everything my life had consisted of had been rendered meaningless at a stroke. With a sure hand death had opened the curtain, and behind it lay the truth in the clearest light: virtually nothing had significance. Almost everything was superfluous. Only dignity was indispensable.

But what I'm doing here no longer has any dignity. It's now been almost two weeks since I last spoke to a living human being. Apart from the walks with Kaja at dusk and the short drives to the nearest supermarket, I haven't left the farmstead. My life makes no sense anymore.

Anybody who thinks that suicide is cowardly is mistaken. It's a hard, courageous, risky act. Failed suicides sometimes end with people needing care and without the slightest chance of recovery. The male methods of hanging or shooting oneself are not for me. A well-mixed cocktail of Vomex, Tavor and Zopiclone is much more up my street and is easier to carry out. I can slit my wrists at the same time.

I sit in the kitchen and look at Kaja. She would start to bark, so I'd have to take her away beforehand, put her in good care, take her to kennels or over to Klaus.

The doorbell rings.

Kaja merely looks up and pricks up her ears. She's waiting for a sign from me. But I don't move. There are a few short, shrill, energetic rings, then two longer ones and one very long ring. The doggedness of the caller rules out Richard, Klaus and the postwoman. I shut Kaja in the kitchen, ignore her whining and howling, and creep to the gate, keeping as close to the wall of the house as possible.

"No, I didn't see her drive off," Klaus says. "She must be around here somewhere."

"Maybe you missed her," a female voice responds, and I recognise Natascha.

"But I've been out here the whole time! Blowtorching the creeping wood sorrel. In front of her house too. She doesn't do it even though I said she should."

Klaus makes the effort to speak high German, especially when pronouncing his verbs. He doesn't omit any letters like he usually does.

Natascha knocks at the gate, calls for me, then keeps ringing the doorbell again. Inside the house Kaja starts barking.

"Aha!" Natascha calls out triumphantly. "The dog!"

"She'll be somewhere at the back of the garden," Klaus speculates, reverting to dialect, but Natascha isn't going to leave it at that.

"What if something's happened to her? I have to go in!"

"My dear lady!" Klaus adopts the tone he uses to bring a discussion to an end. "If the door's shut, it's shut."

He adds, a little more gently, that she shouldn't worry as he's heard me going about my business these last few days. Reluctantly he promises to keep a watchful eye on me and call her if in doubt.

I slowly take a few steps backwards, then turn around, hurry towards the barn, slip through the open sliding door and go all the way to the back, where Frau Adomeit's furniture is stored under covers, and wait. In here there are spiders' webs which are so old that they hang from the beams like closely woven material. Some are huge. If I were to lie them on top of one another they would form a large, white, dusty cloth. Hundreds of spiders have spun these webs, thousands of insects have got caught in them, and I imagine myself suffocating beneath them, disintegrating into dust.

Eventually I venture out of my hiding place, cross the yard and go back inside the house. Kaja greets me as if I'd been away for years. She shakes and howls with delight, writhes, presses herself on the floor, then leaps up again boisterously. Her outburst of joy shames me. Today isn't the day I'm going to go.

13

I'm still here. Out of a mixture of cowardice and a touch of curiosity. It was two days ago that Natascha stood at my gate. I wrote her a long message, inventing a migraine and a tablet-induced sleep with earplugs that neither ringing, knocking nor calling could disturb. I did not fail to mention how touched I was by her concern and how much I appreciate it.

When can I visit you? she wrote back.

As I wait for her I stand by the wall of pictures and lose myself in one of the last photographs of Sonja, which Richard took in the Museum of Fine Arts. Sonja is aping the pose of the bronze sculpture next to her. She's wearing one of my discarded dresses, one that had got too tight around my tummy and only looks good on very young, very slim women – knee-length and red, a circle skirt with a leather belt that Sonja had to punch another hole into. We'd decided to go into the museum on the spur of the moment, to escape the blistering heat. Inside it was cool and quiet, and as we drifted aimlessly through the collection we ended up in a large room where around fifty sculptures were exhibited on pedestals – figurative representations of the human body with technical and artistic precision and expressiveness. Richard's face lit up, especially as we hadn't been expecting anything like this, nor had we seen any notice of the exhibition. When Sonja pointed out the couple to the rear of the room, rolling on the floor and making obscene gestures, Richard looked for a member of staff. A uniformed woman of about sixty was pacing up and down, her hands crossed behind her back, paying no attention to the couple. Now the man rolled on top of the woman, pretended to penetrate her, then rolled off her again. As Richard wandered over to the museum attendant, Sonja and I tried to ignore the couple too, focusing instead on the sculptures that weren't labelled, nor was there any information on the walls. We reckoned most of them dated from the late nineteenth century and I began explaining to Sonja the features that had brought us to this conclusion. Sonja was only listening with one ear; she kept glancing at the couple. "Could we go somewhere else? This is embarrassing."

All of a sudden Richard's laughter resounded through the room. He beckoned us over and explained, shaking his head, that the reason none of the sculptures were labelled was that they were just the background to the actual exhibit, which was the couple on the floor. The bronzes were mere ornamentation, just props.

Later, as we ate in one of our favourite restaurants, we encouraged Sonja to reflect on the thing as a whole, but she didn't want to and kept looking at her phone. I was annoyed by her indifference; my irritation peaked when we bumped into Arvid who, as it turned out, had been to the exhibition too. Unlike Sonja, he immediately got involved in our conversation and, as usual, Sonja hung on his every word.

I take down the photo and put it in a drawer with dozens of others. "You were a really crap mum sometimes," I say out loud.

But I hope I'll be able to forgive myself someday.

*

Natascha and Nina arrive too early. We sit in the garden at the back, where I've given the insects a few square metres of flowers that are running riot. Nina strides purposefully over to the picnic blanket that I've spread out for her, takes off her shoes and tights, and listens to quiet music on her phone. After a brief hesitation Kaja lies beside her. Natascha and I sit on garden chairs a couple of metres away. Her sun-yellow dress is immediately covered in tiny flies.

"What was up last time?" she asks. "I had a really bad feeling."

"Oh, nothing much," I say dismissively. "I was just having a bad day." Then I tell her about Richard and Brida. "Oh," she says, "so that's what's going on." Natascha gives me a stern look. "Ought I to be worried?"

"Not at all."

She nods, pushes her sun hat up and gazes at the sky.

"How's Nina?" I say.

Natascha glances at her daughter, then her eyes widen and stare at a point in the distance. "Let me tell you something," she says below her breath. "From the very start I've been toying with the idea of taking Nina with me when I die."

I gasp. Natascha feebly swipes a few flies from her dress, then clasps her hands on her knees, leans towards me and continues, softly, "The moment I'm no longer here, Nina will be at the mercy of other people, totally defenceless. Even now, when I check on her at least once a week, her carers don't notice if she's got a stone in her shoe and is walking around in pain. It takes them days to work out that she's got toothache, which always ends up in her having dental treatment under general anaesthetic. They don't wash her thoroughly enough after she's been to the loo and don't notice if she gets a vaginal yeast infection days later. I've seen her sitting on a bench in the garden when the temperature's below zero, without a hat and with her coat undone, while the carers are over in the smoking area. They don't clean her ears properly, don't clean the shit from her nails when she's scratched away at her full nappy. They don't challenge her enough. Nina's muscles are wasting away. All those little instances of care and attention that she needs for a halfway healthy and pain-free life are often forgotten. And of course they don't love Nina. Nor will anybody else love her. She'll never have a partner, never have friends. Strangers arrive in eight-hour shifts, and at best they attend to everything that needs doing. But at the end of their shift they shed their responsibility along with their work clothes. Even now there aren't enough staff for all the institutions where people with disabilities live, and it's getting worse by the year. Let's say I make it to eighty. When I die I'll be leaving behind a woman over fifty who suffers from chronic pain, has absolutely zero risk awareness and the intellect of a small child. She'll be a burden on everyone."

Finally Natascha looks at me, but I don't know what to say. I've never seen her so tired and despondent.

"What if more difficult times come?" she whispers. "Water shortages, heatwaves and cold spells, blackouts, war? Nobody will be thinking about people like Nina. All the fuss about integration and inclusion will be forgotten. Everyone will be forced to look after their own, but Nina only has me."

"Do you have any relatives?"

"My parents are over eighty. I don't have any siblings, no husband, no other children and no money. And please don't now ask me if there's anything you can do, because what would that be?"

"But that doesn't mean you can—"

"Yes, I can," she interrupts me. "It might sound horrid, but we're talking about compassion here."

"But," I say, biting the bullet, "doesn't everyone have the right to their own suffering? Look, all of us suffer in one way or another. You, me. Who gives you the right to deny your daughter her own suffering?"

"*I* give myself the right, because there's nothing Nina can learn from it. You and I, Linda, we're in a position to take something from our suffering, grow with it, become better people. But Nina lives only in the moment. And when she suffers – which she will later on – her suffering in that moment will be endless because she won't know that it has an end."

"You're not a Christian, then?"

"You aren't either," she says.

"What makes you think that?"

Natascha smiles. "If you believed in God you'd believe that your child is now in his care. You'd accept your fate and see it as meaningful. But as things stand . . ." She shrugs. "As things stand your daughter's death is pointless, isn't it?"

When I don't respond Natascha apologises. She didn't mean to upset me. Both of us look at Nina, who has put her mobile down and is now singing the start of an old folk song over and over again. Her pleasure wafts through the garden like the summer breeze, touching us.

When she says goodbye at the gate Natascha looks at me in a peculiar way. I'm familiar with the feeling of having said too much, having allowed a stranger to peer too deeply into my personal abyss. It's hard to forgive.

"I understand," I assure her. "Really, Natascha, I understand perfectly well. But there has to be another solution."

Natascha nods without conviction. Nina gently reaches for her mother's hand. Something happens in her pure face and for a moment it is as if she understands. Either she knows nothing or everything, I think, but then the veil that usually surrounds her is back, and she falls into her typical sing-song. The wind carries the sounds in my direction for a while and I watch the two of them walk away until they turn the corner of the road.

I suddenly feel cramped on the farmstead.

At once I shove Kaja into the car and drive eastwards until the landscape begins to change, becoming hillier and more wooded. We park at the foot of a bridge and walk along the riverside path. After a few hundred metres, having not met another soul, only a few waterbirds that Kaja is desperate to hunt, we hear a commotion above us. A flock of squawking crows is flying around another bird. It tries to escape them but the crows are circling it, following each of its manoeuvres. It's a young buzzard which has caught something, perhaps a baby crow. No matter which way it turns the crows prevent it from flying off. They attack the bird, hack at it, screech and squawk, and finally form a billowing black hood from which it cannot escape. The only way out is to head for the ground, where the flock finally rushes at it. Kaja's hunting urge seems to have abated; she stays close to me and doesn't tug on the lead. I watch spellbound as the crows battle the thief, screeching incessantly. Still making a racket they eventually fly back into the air, leaving the buzzard on the ground. We approach it slowly, but Kaja's attention is back on the quacking ducks on the river. I let her off the lead, allow her to trot and hunt and follow her instincts, while I crouch beside the buzzard. It's alive and its yellow-brown eyes are wide open. When I extend a hand towards the bird of prey, it hops away then flies off.

I suddenly feel like running, something I haven't done in years. I can barely manage fifty metres before I'm out of breath, but these are the seconds I've felt most alive in ages.

14

My mother's been ringing every day for the past week. Our conversations are short, simple and without any pretext. She doesn't worry about the effect her words have. Accusations come as easily to her as instructions and lies.

"Hello, Linda," she said this morning, shortly after half past six. "It's your mother here."

"I know," I said.

"I haven't been able to sleep for days." Pause. "You can't go on like this indefinitely." Long pause. "It does my head in every night."

While I was cobbling together an answer she kept going. "I'll tell you this. It's not so easy for a woman going through the menopause to find a man anymore. Women age in bursts, which can be terrifying. You go to bed one night and the following morning you're staring at a stranger in the mirror." She gave a laugh. "You can still save your marriage, Linda," the monologue continued. "And believe me, getting old on your own in a strange place . . ."

"Who says I'm going to get old here? That I'm going to get old at all?"

"Don't you dare give me *that*, Linda!" she cried, incensed. I immediately reassured her.

"I've spoken to Richard," she went on. "He says that this

thing with Brigitta or Britta, or whatever she's called, it's not set in stone."

"Her name is Brida and I bet he never said it in those words to you."

"But that's precisely what he means. He's waiting for you to give him a sign."

"He didn't say that either."

"That's why I'm telling you now."

When I realised that she'd invented the conversation with Richard, I couldn't help but laugh. "I don't find it particularly funny," she said.

For the second time today "Mama" flashes up on my phone screen. It goes to voicemail but she won't leave a message. I weed between the young celery stalks and put three courgette plants into the prepared soil. She'll call again in a few minutes, then again, then yet again until I finally answer.

For years I avoided thinking about my mother. Every thought inevitably took me to a point at which I had to realise that I didn't know this woman. I see her before me in her armour of pore-clogging foundation, red lipstick and dark-brown eye-liner which she draws every day in a juddery line above her almost lash-free lids. She used to be almost beautiful, albeit in a slightly bland way.

She hasn't once been to see me here in the village. She would have to pass by the small town where we used to live and where I drive to at least once a week to shop. Back then it looked dreary and dirty, the small town where my mother lost her parents before I was born. They died in their allotment cabin from carbon monoxide poisoning, the same manner of death that Konrad would later choose. It was an accident, a defective, unauthorised stove inside the cabin. Sitting in their camping chairs, playing cards and drinking beer, they fell unconscious and died. My mother, their only child, remained, seven months pregnant, abandoned by a man who already had a family and didn't even know I was on the way. As the children of Silesian expellees, her parents hadn't become fully rooted. Now my mother was rootless too; she passed seamlessly on to me this feeling of belonging nowhere and being tied to nobody. And then, in a spontaneous, rash act of Herculean will, in which she probably surprised even herself, she turned her back on that small town for ever.

In the summer after the Wall came down, shortly after the customs union, when the state-owned heater factory where she worked in the personnel department was on the verge of closing, she responded to a personal ad in a national newspaper. She circled it with a red pen and I – thirteen at the time – read it, unaware that there would soon be a momentous change in my life. A "handsome, well-to-do banker" from the Rhine–Main area was, "following a major disappointment", looking for a woman to bring "happiness back into his life". My single-parent mother, who for weeks had been suffering from a severe sleep disorder, worried about losing everything she'd believed to be secure and terrified of impoverishment, went to a photographer, had flattering portraits taken and wrote the disappointed, well-to-do man from the West a letter. I never got to read it, of course, but I can keenly imagine its contents. She will have offered herself like a ware that can't be had by everyone. She would have been determined not to "sell herself short" – a phrase I would often hear her say later (when it came to Konrad she didn't sell herself short, she insisted). Evidently she convinced the West German financial adviser of her value at their first meeting. Or was it the rumours circulating at the time about the sexual qualities of women from the East, about their supposed greater modesty and diligence compared to their counterparts in the West? They were said to be emancipated and yet devoted – all-rounders who could effortlessly combine children, household and career, and who got up to the wildest things in the bedroom. Natural children with no shame, unspoiled and malleable. Did my stepfather think these things about my thirty-four-year-old mother? I never found out.

Two and a half months after they met, in the autumn holidays when I was in Year 8, we moved from Saxony to Hessen, to Kronberg in the Taunus.

I can scarcely remember this period of my life. I said goodbye to my friends without realising that I'd never see any of them again. And it didn't occur to me that there wouldn't be any new friendships. Submissively I left my home with my mother and moved into the strange house. It was like we were going on a long trip. Throughout my time in Kronberg I never shook off the feeling that this was temporary, provisional. There were superficial acquaintances, girls who called me their friend, but I didn't experience the sort of friendship you have when you've known somebody all your life and you don't need to explain anything. Each new relationship began with misunderstandings; explanations, ingratiation and submissiveness were always needed. My loneliness was indescribable and my only ally, the link between my old and new lives – my mother – turned her back on me.

With his money, status and supposed intellectual superiority, Konrad domesticated this hitherto independent woman in a remarkably short period of time, got her pregnant almost instantaneously, and then again only a few weeks after my little brother was born. She didn't have to work anymore. Never again. My mother hadn't been expecting this and she realised too late that it was a trap.

What I always gave Konrad credit for was how he embraced me as his daughter. He must have taken this decision very early on, maybe the moment he opted for my mother. In truth he always treated me the same as his biological children. He called me "my girl" or "our Linda" and I received the same financial support and the same attention as my brothers. To begin with this made me suspicious, but evidently it was part of his patriarchal conservatism that I was incorporated into the family construct too, to be held and strengthened, controlled and guided with a firm hand. Whereas my old friends from Saxony had to become adults overnight, because the collapse of the system forced their parents to reinvent themselves, leaving them with no headspace for their teenagers, I took a step backwards into a childhood that, as a typical GDR latchkey kid, I'd never known. The parents from back home didn't smooth any paths, or provide any money or contacts. They didn't get their sons and daughters onto the right internships, didn't pay for trips abroad, no British tennis camps, no art courses in Italy. They were too busy finding ways to combat the humiliation and debasement of their life's achievements, creating new values and digesting the loss of their inner homeland. Whereas I was plucked out of the chaos of this period, taken under the wing of my affluent stepfather and bundled into a school in Kronberg, back home young lives were failing before they even reached the age of adulthood. My adolescent rebellion subsided before it had properly begun. Konrad and my mother made sure that I was busy. School and sport (I had to choose and so plumped for handball) left me no time to go off the rails.

My mother changed. She let her hair grow and copied the way other women dressed. Her voice gradually lost its Saxon brogue, which must have been quite an effort for her. My brothers stayed at home until they were three, then spent half the day at kindergarten, followed by half days at primary school too. It was as if our past had been obliterated. My stepfather wasn't particularly interested in GDR stories; he saw the whole of the East as a developing country and an area for investment. Clearly my mother didn't regard me as a suitable person to discuss her first life with. There was no room in her second life, in which she did everything to erase the traces of the first, for joint memories. She must have suffered from this. I did, at any rate. Apart from the fact that I was barely at home, I virtually stopped talking. When I sat at the dining table with Konrad, my mother and the two boys, I would answer questions in full sentences as requested, but otherwise kept my mouth shut. In those few moments when my mother and I were alone in a room, her gaze would flit past me. Everything about her said: Keep quiet! And I did. I didn't touch on the pain, didn't rouse it. It was almost as if she were afraid of me. For I was the only one who knew the other woman, the one she'd been before, only I saw the contradictions, all that was fake in this new life. Her façade required strength, and my silence helped her to maintain it.

Five missed calls. Doggedness is also a way of showing love, I think, as I dial her number. Instead of greeting me, she says:

"Yes, Linda, I just wanted to tell you that I've found her, that Brida, on the internet. The whole time I was thinking, you know her, you've seen her somewhere before, and then the penny dropped. She did a reading last year in the bookshop here in Kronberg. I even bought one of her books, a crime novel – it's very exciting and well written. She even signed it for me. I've got it here on the shelf."

She leaves a long, meaningful pause. There's something childish about her blatant admiration for people who've "made it", whose names and faces appear in newspapers, magazines and online. "So, if I were in your shoes," she goes on and explains what would be advisable. And I promise her everything. With a satisfied glance at my planted-up vegetable bed I pledge to do whatever she thinks is best. I lie with a soft voice, say "Yes" and "I will", and end the conversation with the certainty that I'm going to have some peace for a few days.

15

In June there's a village festival. As every year, benches and tables are set up on the clubhouse terrace beside the sports field, and there's a covered stage. I'm here for the first time. Klaus caught me this morning on my way back from a walk with Kaja.

"You're coming along this afternoon," he said. Before I could protest, he added, "The Boss said, 'She's got to join in this time.'"

At three o'clock on the dot the two of them are standing, as promised, by the gate. The Boss is wearing a gaudy blouse, which looks cheap but new, and a straight pleated skirt that goes down to her calves. Despite the heat she's also wearing skin-coloured, opaque tights. Klaus smells of aftershave. In his clean jeans and striped shirt he stands stiffly beside his wife.

I sit where they invite me to. A waitress comes over immediately and asks, "What can I get you, my lovelies? Beer? Schnapps? Glass of wine?"

Klaus orders wine for the Boss and me, and a beer for himself.

The residents of the home for the disabled are here too, and those who are able to walk are the first to dance feverishly when the music starts up. The residents in wheelchairs are also pushed onto the dance floor. DJ Rainer gets going.

Schlager numbers are followed by atmospheric music and eighties' hits, and because Klaus has practically downed his first beer in one, the waitress is already back at our table, bellowing, "That glass must have a hole in it! How about I bring you another one, young man?"

"Absolutely!" Klaus replies with a red face, and she shrieks, "Fantastico, my sweetheart." Klaus grins at the waitress and she asks, "Anything else I can do for you?"

"You bet!" Klaus says, and the waitress's shrill laugh irritates the Boss. She grimaces and shoots Klaus a stern look.

The waitress is wearing a Dirndl which her breasts are oozing out of. She greets everyone with a honeyed "Howdy guys!" and says goodbye with a "Ciaoarama!" I'm so mesmerised by her that I've missed the start of the conversation at our table.

"Your average eastern German doesn't do small talk," Klaus is saying with conviction. "He gets straight to the matter in hand. No bullshit, just plain talking. And that's a good thing if you ask me."

"But nobody *is* asking you," the Boss says acidly, taking large gulps of her wine.

Amongst the people from the home, standing on the edge of the dance floor to keep an eye on their charges, I can see Natascha. Her huge straw hat towers over the heads of the others; she's wearing an ankle-length, flowing dress and holding a glass of fizz. Crouching on the ground beside her is Nina, rhythmically hitting the ball of her right hand against her temple. Then she gets up and walks onto the dance floor, waving her arms. Natascha's eyes follow her daughter. Her responsibility for Nina never ends. The relationship between the two is just like it was in the beginning when Nina was a baby. There's no release from the fear and concern. No happy ending.

Now Klaus looks over at Natascha too. This spares me an explanation. I get up and wander over to her, expecting to be greeted by her broad smile. But the expression on her face is negative. There's the hint of a forced smile and she gives me a fleeting hug.

"I didn't think you'd venture out amongst the crowds, Linda."

"It's Klaus's fault," I say, nodding over at our table.

Nina is running back and forth nervously, looking very tense. Natascha straightens her hat and says, "Really quite hot today."

I've never heard Natascha talk about the weather. This big, loud woman, who Klaus says is "a bit too much woman in one go", usually begins conversations without pleasantries. Her detachment bothers me. The last thing we spoke about was Natascha's plan to die with Nina in a murder–suicide. People say these sorts of things, I thought. If this or that happens to me I'll pack it in. If I get dementia please shoot me. If my child dies, that's my life over too. Such talk has no repercussions; nobody means it seriously.

Nina comes prancing over to us, gives her mother a begging look with her large eyes and tries to pull her away.

"It's getting too much for her here," Natascha says. A Schlager is booming from the speakers on either side of the stage.

"We could go to mine, that would make Kaja very happy," I suggest. Natascha hesitates, then agrees. I say goodbye to Klaus and the Boss, who make me promise to come back later.

"That's when it gets really fun," Klaus says. I'm sure he means well by me.

16

The Adomeit daughters' letter is lying unopened on the kitchen table in front of me. I've been staring at it this past half hour since I got back from Leipzig. The envelope is white, the address and sender have been written in a childishly clumsy hand. There's a Mickey Mouse stamp. The letter triggers in me a similar angst as would a communication from the tax authority, the police or the courts. The Adomeit daughters have never written to me before, nor have they ever visited. Gudrun telephoned once to ask if everything was OK with the house, and Renate did too. I haven't seen them since I moved in.

I wasn't here when the post arrived; I was in town. First at the grave, then the white bicycle. In the basket was a bag of dog poo, which I immediately got rid of. I removed all the rubbish from around the bicycle, cleaned the frame and wheels with the hand brush from the car, and filled the basket with fresh flowers. Then I drove into the centre, parked in the underground car park on Augustusplatz and wandered down Grimmaische Strasse. A man was running up and down outside the health and beauty store. He was young, filthy and barefoot, his long, thin hair hung in his face and he was babbling incomprehensibly. Standing not far from him was a woman who was clearly drunk, swearing horribly. She screamed until her face turned red, her arms flung out, and the flow of pedestrians parted around her. Nobody reacted, nobody stopped. I'd forgotten that going mad in the city was an anonymous process and basically there was only one difference between the two of them and me: I didn't lose control.

I bought toothpaste, floss, sun cream and a hairbrush with wild boar bristles, feeling amazed by my unexpected desire for body-care products, then at the till reached almost friskily for a packet of melon chewing gum. In the nearest bookshop I bought a book. I ate a scoop of vanilla ice cream in a cone and was briefly tempted to go into the small boutique on Thomaskirchhof, where I often used to buy my clothes. The shop owner, who was putting up a new window display, stopped what he was doing and looked at me. A smile appeared on his lips and when he raised his hand in greeting I ducked my head and hurried on.

The drive back to the village took longer than expected. Following a diversion, the road led me into an area on the outskirts of Leipzig where I'd once gone to evaluate an artist's estate. When I spotted the house I slowed to walking pace. I recalled that I'd always felt a particular happiness, independent of Richard and Sonja, whenever I was given the chance to browse prints, drawing, sketches, when I touched sculptures, rearranged large pictures, placed them on their own, turned the spotlight on them – in short, whenever art touched my life.

Living in that house was a sick, lonely and impoverished woman, hoping to find a home for her artworks before she died. I had to disappoint her.

The estates of female artists often came with tragic stories. There were many artist couples, but the women had usually been less successful than their male partners. They'd looked after the children and the household, and given their husbands the feeling of being more important than themselves, even when, in the evening, having seen to all their other obligations, they created really good art in some corner of the their home. In most cases the foundation did nothing more than inspect the works. Sometimes I advised the heirs, recommending that they catalogue everything and offer it to an auction house. Each time I wished I could do more, but only once did I buy a woman's entire estate and included the best of her pictures in one of our exhibitions that showcased the perspectives of female artists in the last years of the GDR.

Now the house was deserted, the windows boarded up and people were hooting insistently behind me. I put my foot down, drove out of the city and thought that there had been a life without Sonja. Viewed from a notional day in the future, motherhood will have constituted the lesser portion of my life. It was possible that the greater part still lay before me.

When I got back, Kaja didn't meet me at the gate as usual. The only thing in my mailbox was the Adomeits' letter. I went inside, put the envelope on the table and squatted beside the dog, who seemed to be asleep on her blanket. She raised her head, blinked weakly then closed her eyes again.

Now I'm sitting here, covering the letter with both hands and wondering whether the cramp-like pain in my stomach is down to the dog's odd behaviour or the contents of the envelope. I look at Kaja. Of late she's been trotting half-heartedly down the arid, cracked paths across fields and through woods. Yesterday she ate badly and this morning I noticed an imbalance in the way she was moving, a slight limp.

"What do you think, Kaja? Shall I open the letter?"

She makes a sound but doesn't move.

I open the envelope, pull out a single sheet of paper, read it word for word, then put it on the table. A dull throbbing in my head forces me to sit very still. I glance down at Kaja, whose eyes are still closed. Her breathing appears shallow. The gentle rising and falling of her body seems to have a different rhythm from normal.

"Think of the rule!" I command myself. "Just because it's going badly, that doesn't mean it can't get worse."

I look up the address of the nearest vet and drive Kaja there.

"You remind me of someone," the vet says, looking at me pensively. The effort makes her lined face look even more wrinkled. Hairs are sprouting above her narrow lips and her short grey hair lies flat on her head.

"I remember!" she cries. "There was this friend I used to have at school . . ."

She says my mother's name.

"She had a daughter, but then they left. That must have been not long after the Wall came down. She didn't come back to the school reunion either. Nobody had an address for her. You're not by any chance her—?"

"No, no, I don't come from here," I reply.

I've no desire to talk. On another day, in different circumstances, I'd ask her a thousand questions, but now the diagnosis with all its consequences is hanging in the air. In my head I think what she hasn't yet said. That there's the option of putting Kaja to sleep if her pain becomes unbearable, if she stops eating and drinking. That she doesn't have to suffer endlessly, that we can deliver her from that.

The time she has left corresponds with the deadline the Adomeit daughters have given me. I'm going to have to leave the village in less than three months. Without Kaja.

In bed, for the first time in ages, I wish I had someone here with me, a good, calm person to help me through the night. I struggle to breathe, my heart beats at twice its normal speed, stops, then races again and sweat runs between my breasts. My nightie sticks to my body; I have to take it off and get another one.

Life is a series of farewells, I think, and all of these are a preparation for the final farewell. I think of Nina and Natascha's desperate plan, Konrad's asphyxiation in his car, my grandparents in their cabin, and then I think of Sonja. I should never have allowed her to cycle to the gynaecologist that day. I ought to have taken her doubts about the pill seriously. What was the worst that could have happened? A child, that's what could have happened. To prevent a child I let my daughter go down a path she didn't want to, and which was her last.

With trembling hands I push a second Zopiclone from the blister pack, swallow it without water, place a Tavor on my tongue and, after a few minutes, feel the fear slowly subside and sleep approach.

PART TWO

1

Here used to be my home.

This is where we lived – my husband, my child and I. That was my family.

Everything is spick and span. Even the windows have been cleaned. The fridge door is open; it's empty and has been switched off. In the bedroom the bed is only made on Richard's side; on my side the colourful throw is folded up.

The door to Sonja's room is closed.

I hope I don't have to wait too long for him. *Running slightly late,* he wrote a quarter of an hour ago. All the pictures are still on the walls, drawings and prints that Richard and I collected during our life together, as well as a selection of his own pictures. I look at them as if I were at an exhibition, pretend that I'm not in my own flat, that I'm seeing all these works of art for the first time. There are some outstanding pieces here and the total value of the collection must run into the tens of thousands. If we were to sell the art along with the flat we could ask for more, at least three-quarters of a million euros. Back then we snapped up the flat without thinking too long about it. The asking price was well below today's property prices. Thanks to what I'd inherited, the amount we still needed was manageable, and because of my job we easily secured a mortgage, which has been paid off in the meantime.

There are lots of things we did right, Richard and I.

"Sorry," he calls out when he enters the flat. "This city is one big building site."

His embrace is coy, almost fleeting. He's wearing trendy branded trainers with jeans and an expensive-looking shirt. He looks really good.

His eyes dart to the door of Sonja's bedroom.

"I haven't been in," I say.

"Nothing's changed."

"Are you living at Brida's?" I ask.

"Most of the time, yes. For some reason it wasn't working out here. I didn't feel comfortable with her. Besides, her younger child is still at home and needs her."

"How old is she?"

Richard hesitates before answering and runs a hand across his brow. "Undine's twenty already," he says, as if it were a stigma to still be living at home at that age.

He hangs up his coat and goes into the kitchen. I follow him and then we sit facing each other at our old dining table. Outside the magnolia bends in the wind. Neither of us fetches anything to drink, neither offers the other anything. We're strangers in our own flat.

Richard listens to me and doesn't protest when I suggest selling it.

No attempt to make me change my mind. No *we* anymore.

"I think seven hundred thousand is realistic," he says, and I can't help smiling because our estimates are so similar.

"What are you planning to do now?" he asks.

"Don't know," I say with a shrug. "I mean, the dog's still alive."

"Why don't you have her put to sleep?"

I can't believe he's just said that. I get up, go to the window and look down at the bike racks.

"I'm not going to have the dog put down until her pain becomes unbearable," I say without turning to Richard.

"Oh, sure. Sorry."

Our discussion about how to divide up the various tasks passes without further incident. It might be a year before the flat is sold. I'm not bothered, I've got the time. Richard, on the other hand, is suddenly displaying an urgency that assails me.

We arrange to meet again as soon as Richard has found a suitable estate agent. He accompanies me to the door like a random guest and gives me a slightly more heartfelt hug than when he arrived, but it's lacking the old warmth. Then the door to the flat closes behind me and I stand in the stairwell like an abandoned animal.

For a moment I don't know what to do.

I can hear footsteps down below. Gentle, springy footsteps. Young legs always taking two steps at a time. All of a sudden I'm certain that Sonja's head, with its high, bobbing ponytail, is about to appear before me. I'm going to see the shock on her face because the noise-cancelling headphones mean she only notices me at the last moment. My heart pounding, I hurry towards the footsteps and, one landing below, bump into a young man I've never seen before.

When I'm in the street I stare at the bike stand. This is where her bicycle was; I could have stopped her here. From the open window upstairs I could have shouted, "Wait, Sonja. Let's talk about it. There are other options." Instead I was on the phone to an architectural practice, explaining the conditions for renting one of our foundation's rooms. They were planning a champagne reception with a DJ and finger food, and needed a projector and screen for a presentation. For about eight minutes I spoke to a determined woman who tried to negotiate the fair price down further. At the end of our conversation, when we'd reached an agreement, Sonja must have been close to the scene of the accident.

I didn't feel anything at the moment of her death. No sixth or seventh sense made me flinch, no hunch sent my pulse racing. Even when the hospital rang I took the call unsuspectingly.

Blinded by tears I drive through the city. I steer the car aimlessly behind others, turn onto the ring road that circles the inner city, pass the Gewandhaus and opera house and wonder: Who am I now, without a husband, without a child, without a job? I take the exit to head north, back to the village, Kaja and the chickens. But that's over too. What am I going to do with myself now? People with children have a meaning to their life. People with a job have a meaning to their life. People with both survive death twice.

There's nothing left of a person like me.

2

For my move back to Leipzig I hired the Syrian man who'd cleared out the farmstead. He remembered me at once. "Oh, lady in village, yes, yes."

"Back to husband?" he said on the phone.

I laughed and he said no more.

While the young men, who still can't speak a word of German, are installing the wardrobe in my new flat, he's having a cup of tea with me in the kitchen.

I ask him if he feels happy in his house in Thuringia. If he likes living in Germany. A crooked, indecisive smile twitches on his face and he rocks his head from side to side.

"Germany broken," he says. "Families broken. Old people alone, woman with children alone, no strong family, no strength," he says, then adds, "Different with us. Not alone. Family strong."

Every word is like a slap. He knows nothing about me and yet knows everything. I wish he'd leave. In the bedroom something falls crashing to the ground. He frowns, calls out a few words in Arabic, then turns back to me. His face is flexible, his expression continually changing. Only when he looks at me does he radiate a confidence-building harmlessness.

"Need invoice?" he suddenly asks, in a way that encourages a "No" on my part. I shake my head, wondering how often he does this. Then he finishes his tea and lends a hand. Under his vigilant gaze the lads work their way swiftly from room to room. The relationship between them is a puzzle. They respect and fear him, I can see that. They don't take breaks, never look at me and say little.

At the end of the day a bundle of cash makes its way into the Syrian man's coat pocket and the lads get an extra tenner from me each. The cupboards are up, the sink in the kitchen is working, the washing machine is plumbed in, and I'm standing in my new bedroom surrounded by cardboard boxes. I look out of the window into the rear courtyard, which is half paved, half laid to lawn, and bordered by a screen fence covered with ivy. I've finally given up the old idea of my life. Step by step, day by day, I'm inching forwards. It's not more than that, but it doesn't have to be any more either.

Kaja was buried two weeks ago, in the garden beneath the old lilac bush. The new owners have taken possession of the house, garden and chickens. Just before I left I invited Klaus and the Boss, and Gunhild with her husband and mother to a farewell dinner. As Gunhild fed her tiny, old mother crumbs of the butter cake, she told me I was better off in the city than out here.

"Why?" I asked her.

"What you've got here is nothing. All alone. It makes you go strange."

Klaus nodded and advised me to get a man. "You're not an old bag yet!" he said, and the Boss added, "Not like me!"

She grunted a laugh and Gunhild, glancing at her mother with dementia, said soberly that Klaus was right because someone would have to look after me too. Let's face it, we were all going to get old.

"But statistically men die earlier than women," I pointed out, and they all said in unison, "Oh, right . . . well . . ."

The Boss patted Klaus's knee and he asked for a schnapps. My hope that this dinner wouldn't go on too long came to nothing. We were still at the table until just before midnight, and by the end I was laughing as I hadn't done in years.

Unexpectedly this made my move away easier than I'd imagined, not harder. I'd never thought my story in the village through to its end. Now it stopped so abruptly that there was no room for regret.

A few days after my little celebration, Kaja died. That morning I'd been unable to give her the medicine because she wasn't eating or drinking. She peed and shat in the kitchen, was unsettled, and when I went to fetch the bucket and mop she escaped outside, dragging herself to the chicken enclosure. I let her in and she found a place by the fence, in a small hollow. She never got up again.

Apart from brief visits to the loo and a swift lunch in the kitchen, I stayed close to her. Maybe I imagined it, but over the course of the difficult hours that day almost all the chickens went over to her one last time. The brave ones hopped onto her emaciated body and she didn't resist. At dusk it came to an end. Kaja's breathing was shallow and rapid, and then she wasn't breathing anymore. I took the hens into their house and carried Kaja back to the kitchen, where I laid her carefully on a nest of blankets. I closed her eyes, brushed her fur, washed her muzzle with a lukewarm cloth and lay down beside her, while outside night fell and a late summer's full moon rose.

To begin with my tears came in a gentle trickle, then I was rocked by one sobbing fit after another. I cried for hours on end. I wandered around, screaming, kicking furniture, throwing things against walls and making excruciating sounds that seemed to come from the deepest layers of grief.

The next day I buried Kaja. On her grave I planted a collection of flowering bulbs. The following spring the new owners of the house would enjoy crocuses, narcissi and tulips, without knowing what the plant roots were feeding on.

The sparrows are being noisy in the ivy on the screen wall when a text arrives from Natascha. Would I be free in an hour? She had something important to discuss. *Yes, of course,* I write back.

I watch her prowl around my flat, scrutinising everything with unashamed curiosity. The large kitchen, the two similar-sized rooms, then the bathroom and back into the kitchen, where she opens the door to the balcony, peers out, then closes the door again immediately.

"Ghastly, that screen fence," she says.

We drink golden milk, which I've made with ginger, turmeric, cinnamon and pepper.

"I've found a place for Nina in southern Germany," she says. "In a village in the Black Forest, an anthroposophic community where people with and without disabilities live and work together. We had three trial days that went incredibly well, and now we've secured the place." With an absent-minded expression she stirs three teaspoons of honey into her milk. "They've even got a choir Nina's going to sing in," she continues, and I can't hear the slightest hint of pleasure in her voice.

"Southern Germany . . . That's quite a long way away."

"But it's a great set-up. They look at people differently, Nina won't just be a burden there. It can't go on any longer here. They put her to bed at half past six, a grown young woman! She spends twelve hours in that shitty bed. Twelve hours! Her wounds don't heal anymore because she keeps opening them. She's forever scratching out of sheer boredom, and when I asked the management to file her fingernails so they were short and round, they told me they didn't have time for such frippery. And Nina's not singing anymore. Can you imagine that? My daughter without any singing? She's regressing! I have to provide all the stimulation and entertainment myself, but I can't do it anymore. It's as simple as that, Linda. I – can't – do – it – anymore. This hollow drivel about inclusion . . . The reality is quite different. In real life Nina is picked up by a driver in the morning, put in a car with dark-tinted windows so nobody can see what's going on behind them, taken to educational daycare, where she's kept pretty safe, then driven back to the home in the afternoon, where they feed and wash her and put her to bed far too early."

She reaches for a pencil on the table beside my notepad, twists up her wild hair and fixes the knot with it.

"But the Black Forest," I argue again, "that's at least a six-hour drive away."

"That's why I'm going to move near her for the time being. I've already found someone to rent the flat, but there's the garden." She looks at me expectantly. "It's just five minutes from here by bike. There's a cabin and tools, the whole shebang."

A jolt shoots through my body. Natascha's request seems like a lifeline.

"Yes," I say without hesitation. "I'll gladly look after the garden." Then I hear myself say, "Thanks for thinking of me, Natascha, it's so kind of you."

Throwing her hands theatrically in the air, Natascha says, "If you knew how long I've been waiting for you to let your guard down!"

"Am I such bad company?"

"Not at all. But you're the most aloof person I've ever met." She smiles, gets up and wanders around the table. "Let's have a hug."

For a moment I doubt the necessity of this new-found intimacy. It feels as if Natascha now has an open invitation to turn up at my door unannounced. But there's so much warmth in her embrace that I wish it would never end.

We wheel our bicycles to the garden and I watch Natascha as she speaks. Every emotion finds expression on her face – the anticipation of Nina's new living community, her worry about money because she doesn't have any work there yet, her fear of a long, lonely winter in a strange place. I keep my thoughts to myself. The idea of accommodating Nina in a remote village in a closed community brings forth terrible images in my head. If just one of the carers abuses their power. Just one—

I recall one of those silly sayings that my mother regularly sends me: *Comparison is the thief of joy*. But only if we come off worse. Then we envy them, the cleverer ones, the more beautiful ones, those with healthy children, those in love, the successful, the rich and the talented. On the other hand, a reverse comparison enhances our own lives. The losses and defeats of others allow us to appreciate once more what we've taken for granted. I'm not free of this either. I see Natascha walking bolt upright next to me, with her unwieldy town bike, and I'm grateful that I don't have to go down her difficult path. And at a stroke I know that, for the time being at least, I'm not going to contact any of my old friends. I'm not going to give anyone the opportunity to realise how lucky they are by taking stock of my loneliness and grief. I don't want to envy anyone anything and I don't want anyone to feel sorry for me.

Nobody's going to get the chance to look at me as I'm looking at Natascha.

We've arrived. Natascha unlocks the gate to the allotments and locks up again behind us. She stops at plot number 17 – a well-tended and well-structured garden at the end of a path named Rosengasse – puts the bike down and says with a sigh, "Well. Here we are."

Once again I'm taking over something that another woman is leaving behind. Soon I'll be harvesting quinces and apples from trees I haven't planted, mulching plants, digging beds. I'll fill the birdhouse with food, turn off the water before the first frost and close the cabin shutters. In spring I'll watch the garden come to life, prune, replant and sow. Like most people I'll enjoy the eternal circle of growth and decay.

My attention is drawn to the garden to the right. All the tough plants have spread uncontrolled. Ivy has wrapped itself around the measly apple tree, ferns surround the cabin, fat hen has colonised an entire bed, while nettles, ground elder, thistles, dandelions and thorn apple are rampant. Natascha says that the plot was reallocated recently but she doesn't know who the new tenants are. Silently I hope they'll be people without children.

"And are you sure you'll cope?" Natascha says. The "you'll" sounds like a jarring note in an otherwise harmonious piece of music.

"Absolutely," I say. "I had a bigger garden in the village."

She instructs me in how to use the wood chipper, shows me the water point and fuse box, explains the compost bins and gives a brief summary of allotment regulations in Saxony.

"You have to stick to them," she says. "Developers are hanging around here, reporting any infringements. If the allotment association loses its status, all this is at risk."

Back outside the gate she hands me the second set of keys, which she's brought along as a precaution, gives me a tight hug and promises to be in touch.

"Trust your instinct," I say. "If something down there seems funny, come back with Nina. There'll be another solution somehow."

She nods feebly, then we cycle off in different directions.

3

In retrospect I conclude that all these things had to happen. First Grete Admoeit, Kaja and the farmstead, then the friendship with Natascha and Nina, and now the garden. The garden rescues me from the emptiness of my days. Everything falls into place; I don't have to do anything.

In the first few weeks after my move, I give structure to my days and sound out the neighbourhood.

On the ground floor of my new building there are two flatshares whose tenants seem to change continually. These young people all wear similar clothes and their reluctance to say hello is pretty uniform too.

Right beside me lives an elderly couple who interact with such familiarity, as Richard and I might have done too if our relationship hadn't foundered before its time. I often find the husband standing on the pavement outside, peering nervously down the street.

"I'm expecting my wife," he says as soon as he sees me. I promise that if I bump into her I'll say she has to hurry home because he's worried about her. Each time his "Thank you!" comes from the bottom of his heart, and I always think: If one of these two dies, the other will follow on quickly. The wife, a short, very slim and upright woman, is still light on her feet and climbs the stairs almost as quickly as I do. They're both professors and love music, as I can hear on the balcony from their open windows. Beethoven, Schubert and Mahler are their favourites.

Below me lives a short, fat man with two long-legged, lean greyhounds, under-exercised, nervy, magnificent-looking animals that in their natural environment would hunt their prey on sight, whereas now the most they manage is to urge their puffed-out owner around the neighbouring park. He goes out with them several times a day, always panting and with a bright-red face when he returns. Occasionally a similar-looking man comes round, his brother perhaps, and then they take the dogs for a walk together.

Apart from the dog owner there's another man who lives on his own. He's about forty and has a nondescript face. From time to time his children come to visit, two adolescent girls, the elder of which, with her stork-like legs and high ponytail, reminds me of Sonja. I never see her without headphones and in the lonely eyes of her father I recognise the silent acquiescence I've noticed in many parents who see their children only occasionally. Happiness looks different.

The only child living in the building belongs to the couple in the attic flat. Under his mother's supervision the little boy often scoots around the courtyard on his balancing bike, climbs up a tiny red-and-blue plastic slide, slithers down and is scooped up by his mother. She says the name of everything he touches or looks at, articulating every syllable. When he looks up, she says, "That is the sky, the birds and aer-o-planes fly up there." When he's on his balancing bike, she says, "You are ri-ding your ba-lanc-ing bike." When he plays in the sandpit she picks up the plastic moulds and says, "Muss-el, Flow-er, Bee-tle." When he runs up the stairs, she says, "Don't run up the stairs!" On one occasion I see him standing in the courtyard beside his father. A remote-controlled car shoots across the tarmac, goes crashing into the screen fence, flips over and then keeps going. The boy reaches for the remote control which his father is holding. "Papa, Papa, Papa. Me too!" The father steers the car forwards, backwards, forwards, backwards, with a contented smile on his face. The boy cries and throws his arms out in vain; his father doesn't notice him. He's a paediatric surgeon, I learn from my neighbour.

Nobody in this building is going to get too close to me. We'll greet, pass and forget each other. Nobody will look after anyone else. We could even die unnoticed.

I've soon organised my daily sorties. Within a radius of around five hundred metres from my flat I can find everything I need to live: grocery, organic shop, bank, two bakeries, a chemist, medical centre and a bookshop. If I were to put the dots on a map and join them up, I would end up with a shape looking like a three-pointed crown. I avoid the large supermarket. The small organic shop, a tiny weekly market outside the church on Saturdays and the baker on the corner are enough.

The memorable encounter at the baker's takes place in my second month. A queue has formed outside the shop; I join the end of it. I'm the only person not staring at their phone. Instead I read the slogans on the shop windows: *Thoroughbread. Glorye. Rolliable. Bunanza.* I don't envy the person who spends their days thinking these things up.

A slender girl approaches. The black tears beneath her eyes, three on either side, have been tattooed on. Now that she's right beside me there's no doubt. It's Freya, Sonja's best friend.

"Hey," she says timidly, pushing back her hood. I can make out a dark zigzag pattern in her hair which has been shaven short at the sides, her ears are full of piercings, she smells of cigarette smoke and coughs a few times.

"How are you?" she says with a raw voice.

"Still alive," I reply.

"Me too!" she says proudly, smiling.

Tears gather behind my eyes. How many holidays did she spend with Sonja, Richard and me, how often did she eat at ours, stay the night? I'd love to give her a hug, but I sense a barrier that wasn't there before.

There's building work on the road beside us. A welder switches on his device and Freya looks wide-eyed into the blazing white light.

"Don't look!" I say. "You'll ruin your eyes!"

She shrugs, blinks and says, "I haven't seen you in ages. What are you doing here?"

"I live around the corner."

"Really? You and Richard—"

"No, only me," I interrupt her.

"Oh, right," she says. "I live here too. In a flatshare."

Before I can ask she tells me about her parents' separation, their new partners and how she, Freya, no longer features in their lives. When I say I can scarcely believe that, she was always the most important thing as far as her parents were concerned, Freya interrupts me.

"You don't need to defend them. They wouldn't do that for you." When I raise my eyebrows she adds, "They didn't say nice things about you, in the beginning when you spoke to everyone about Sonja and when Niklas and I were round at your place all the time. They found it "totally intrusive", said you were completely obsessive, letting yourself go and taking everyone with you."

"Oh . . . they said that?"

"And that they totally felt sorry for your husband."

"Uh-huh."

"I've broken off contact with them," she adds in a flat voice. "My parents and me, it just doesn't work."

As we progress in the queue I try to hide my horror at this. Freya must have noticed my stolen glances at her black tears. "I don't regret them," she says defiantly. "Besides, I can always have them lasered later. The guy at the tattoo studio said that black's easier to get rid of. Better than light colours."

"What are you crying about?"

Freya looks at me in disbelief. "About the whole fucked-up world, of course."

"OK," I say, immediately annoyed by my useless answer.

Then it's my turn. I buy a spelt loaf and a baguette, and ask Freya what she needs. While she talks to the assistant my gaze falls on her threadbare cloth bag, covered in stickers. *Girls run the world. My body, my choice. Fuck CO2. There is no planet B. Fuck the AfD. Fish lives matter. Fuck the Police. Fuck them all. FCK NZS. This is what a feminist looks like.*

I watch Freya drop a bun, a poppy-seed roll, two croissants and half a wheat and rye loaf into her bag of fury, then pay for both of us.

Outside the shop she lights a cigarette and inhales deeply.

"Thanks for the stuff. Really kind of you," she mumbles. "I've got to go."

She pulls the hood back over her head, puts the bag over her shoulder and marches off. I watch until she turns the corner at the next junction.

The encounter leaves me baffled. Freya's life hasn't stood still. The change in her seems like another erasure of my daughter. The young woman with the black tears beneath her eyes no longer has anything to do with Sonja's effervescent friend.

On the way home I wonder if Sonja would have taken a similar path. Whether she would have mutilated her appearance and brought her fuck-messages out into the world. Whether she would have been capable of breaking off contact from us. Whether, in her eyes, it no longer worked between us.

I summon the memory of the old Freya – the courageous, confident, sometimes disagreeably precocious Freya. Who – as I once said to Richard – was at the right school, unlike Sonja. Her lively intellect absorbed knowledge with ease, whereas from Year 10 onwards Sonja needed help in almost all the sciences. In their friendship Freya was ever the dominant one. Sonja was always in her slipstream and, from time to time, she'd be unusually funny, cheeky and boisterously silly. She benefited from Freya's energy; Richard and I always believed that Sonja was more dependent on Freya than the other way round, but perhaps that – like so much else – was a fallacy.

4

I saw Esther today. When I stepped out of the organic shop I spotted her on the other side of the street, wandering hand in hand with a man towards the chemist's. It was the wind-turbine millionaire. So the relationship had lasted. Esther didn't look in my direction and I did nothing to attract her attention.

We'd met each other by chance once before, after a long time. Before my mother and I moved to Kronberg in the Taunus, Esther and I were in the same class, sat together in lots of lessons and met up frequently after school. When I moved away, however, we lost contact. Many years later we bumped into each other at Leipzig market. I had Sonja in a sling and was at a stall that sold bread, oil and pesto, which was supposedly run by members of the Twelve Tribes, a sect that believed corporal punishment was part of a child's education. My conscience wrestled with my desire for the excellent bread, and I scrutinised the faces of both sellers – a woman and a man – for signs of wickedness. But I couldn't find anything. Just as I was about to buy a loaf, an incredibly beautiful woman came up to me and said my name loudly and joyfully.

In the first few weeks after our reunion we met up all the time. Esther lived alone just a few streets away from us, and worked in film as a director's assistant. She had no children, but that wasn't by choice. Esther suffered from endometriosis and had been ditched by her boyfriend for a woman who bore him three children. Despite this it didn't seem to be a problem for her that I had a baby.

Esther knew things about my childhood that I couldn't remember. She recalled my mother, as a member of the local workers' collective, being at school when our reports were handed out in Year 4 and presenting Esther with a certificate because she was the best in the class. She reminded me of how often I'd missed school because I was a sickly child, and thus how often my name had been called out before lessons when a pupil would stand in front of the class and report absentees. She imitated the announcement that always ended with the Pioneer greeting; this unleashed a cascade of memories. Faces, voices, places emerged from the darkness of the past and played out in my mind like a badly cut film. She also imitated my mother with remarkable accuracy, the way she always used to say, "No, not inside! Children belong in the fresh air," if we wanted to play in my room when the weather was bad. That hardly ever happened. She told me about the time in Year 6 when I won a recitation competition with Schiller's ballad "The Cranes of Ibycus", her victory in a maths olympiad, our teachers and their idiosyncrasies, Saturday lessons, the Subbotniks, practice drills and how to tell a fire alarm from a chemical alarm, and a chemical alarm from an air raid. Also how her mother bitched about mine because she "made eyes" at married men and had "trysts" with some of them, which I could hardly believe. By telling me all of this, Esther gave me a part of my life back, which my mother seemed to have erased with her silence. Everything was still there and from now on Esther was the link to it. Fragmented individual images became whole sequences. I saw my mother dusting the ornamental cups that decorated our wall unit, beating out the rugs in the courtyard, polishing the floorboards in our flat, almost all of which were cracked. I saw her in her apron opening a tin of fish in our kitchen – herring fillet in tomato sauce – and stirring sugar and lemon into peppermint tea. Far too much sugar. I saw her put on make-up and open one of the doors of the mirrored wardrobe to check her haircut at the back. I saw her go out in the evening in her best shoes and best beige coat, but I never knew where. I saw myself staying up, pushing a chair to the window, with a blanket around me that she'd knitted herself, waiting anxiously for her to return. Without her I would be all alone. There were only the two of us and that – as I'd been well aware for ages – was too few.

Esther joined my memories together and for a while I was properly addicted to listening to her stories. To begin with I regularly invited her to our flat. When there was a bigger group of us she was usually there too. Esther was entertaining and knew all the gossip from the film sets. Besides, her beauty enhanced any occasion. Everyone liked looking at her. Only later, when Sonja reached preschool age, did I see her less often. Richard wasn't a fan of Esther. "She's vulgar," he once said. He didn't like her short, peroxided hair, her assertive manner, the way she didn't mince her words, calling a spade a spade. He despised the way she spoke about men, saying that if he or one of his mates talked about women in a similar vein there would be uproar. In truth I rarely heard Esther talk about men without biting sarcasm, but excused it on account of her painful experience of being dumped in favour of a woman who could have children.

"Just imagine I couldn't have given you a child. Wouldn't you have gone looking for a fertile man?"

"Yes, I probably would have," I replied truthfully.

Esther wasn't popular with Sonja either. Once Sonja was in tears over her houseplant, a small monstera. The leaves hung limply even though the soil was damp, and Sonja sobbed as she whispered something into my ear. She thought the plant had died because she sometimes threw her bogies in the pot. I don't know why, but I told this to Esther, who laughed out loud and said, "What nonsense!" From that day on Sonja would hide away in her room whenever Esther turned up.

Our friendship persisted, however. She knew things about me that nobody else could know apart from my mother. I saw her love affairs come and go, sometimes envying her the thrill, the hormone rush and the euphoria of the new, but never the loneliness and fear she also admitted – the fear of dying alone, becoming cranky and not realising it, the fear of poverty in old age and long, lonely years in some understaffed care home. It was beyond my imagination that someday I would be the one terrified of all of this.

Occasionally when I came home after one of our meetings, I would give Richard a hug and keep telling him how much I loved him. He would then ask, "What's up? Is everything OK?" My answer would be to kiss him and feel grateful that I didn't have to lead a life like Esther's.

When Sonja died, Esther had just started caring for her mother, who was paralysed on one side of her body following a stroke. Esther had no siblings and so was the only person able to do this. For a while Esther would pop in having spent several hours with her mother. She wasn't in a good way and because of this I was glad when she came and the leaden heaviness in our flat, paired with another heaviness, curiously becoming lighter as a result.

*

When Esther and her companion enter the chemist's I hurry down the street to the next junction, turn the corner and breathe again. A few minutes later I open the mailbox in our stairwell, take out an envelope that's been redirected to my new address and stare in disbelief at the name of the sender. It's Esther. In her barely legible handwriting she writes about how she misses our friendship and reveals her anxiety about getting in touch with me. She tells me about all the messages she's typed on her phone before deleting them, about letters she's begun that end up in the wastepaper basket, and announces that she's getting married next summer. The party is at Villa Hasenholz and I'm invited.

I flee up the stairs to the sanctuary of my own four walls.

If I died and strangers came into my flat they'd be confronted by a puzzle. I haven't arranged or decorated anything. Everything is functional, plain and without individual character. I could easily rent the flat on Airbnb. I've turned all the seats to face the windows. I'll alternate between looking at the screen fence in the courtyard or the plane tree in the street. *You can't live like this,* I hear my mother say.

During the days that follow my gaze keeps sweeping Esther's letter, which is on the chest of drawers in the hallway. Eventually, however, it's covered by advertising material and other post, and I forget that it exists.

Bit by bit I fetch the remaining stuff from the old flat whose sale is as good as concluded. I pile the boxes by my empty sitting-room wall. The only things I unpack are Sonja's, which are given a place on a table in the bedroom. Her yearly planner, in which she'd often written her meetings and activities retrospectively, her hairbrush with hair in it, the leather pencil case, her favourite jumper of pink mohair and her jewellery. The books she read over and over again, concert and cinema tickets, notebooks with scribblings and little pictures accompanying the writing, photos, her school ID and an old, chewed piece of gum in a tissue.

Richard calls regularly, asks how I'm doing and what I need. In each of these questions I can hear his bad conscience. If I do actually express a wish he often responds to it that same day. I hate his pity and am almost pleased that someone has taken on him and his needs.

I spend most of the day in Natascha's garden, regardless of the weather. I mulch the flower beds with leaves, fertilise the lawn, harvest apples and quinces, gather up rotten windfall and bury it in a hole. I dig over empty beds, working in fresh compost and clean the cabin. An extraordinarily large spider keeps popping out from behind the cupboard. I'm neither disgusted nor scared and I talk to it like an old friend. I send Natascha a raft of photos as proof of my hard work, as well as a video of the spider. She replies, telling me not to kill the spider, which has been there for a while. On one occasion I meet the old tenant of the neighbouring plot. She's just here to remove her things from the cabin, she calls over to me. Then she steps up to the fence and the expression on her face invites me to come closer too. Without being asked she tells me about the three husbands she's buried and the three children she never gave birth to. Three times she was pregnant, three times she lost the child and then it didn't work anymore. Three was not her lucky number. Now she's old, eighty-two, too frail for gardening, but recently she's fallen in love.

"The love thing," she says with an incredulous laugh, "it never stops."

"Who's taking over your garden?" I ask.

"A couple. About your age. She's nice. He . . ." She makes a dismissive gesture. "He doesn't say much."

"Do they have children?"

"There weren't any with them."

Then, suddenly in a hurry, she puts the full sack of rubbish over her shoulder, turns around when she's at the gate and calls out, "Where's your husband?"

"Don't have one," I call back.

"What? But you're so good-looking! Go and find yourself one. You need a husband for the garden."

She doesn't wait for an answer. I turn to get on with my work and think that these sorts of people are my favourite, the ones who touch my life like beams of light at the side of the road.

Sometimes I'll go into one of the few cafés where my nerves aren't overloaded by loud music and leaf through the newspapers. Occasionally I'll get absorbed in an interview and forget the other customers around me until a waiter or waitress comes up and asks if everything's alright or if I want anything. I'd love to respond to this "Is everything alright?" with a "Nothing's alright, absolutely nothing", but I stick to the rules, smile and answer, "Yes, thank you." If I look up I often see myself surrounded by young mothers in sporty clothing, feeding their babies and patting their backs afterwards while on the phone, until the burp comes. Then they lift their little one in the air until the nappy is by their nose and they sniff at it like animals, before disappearing into the bathroom with child and changing stuff, while the waitress serves another chai latte with almond milk.

That's when I usually leave.

It's not the feeding that bothers me, nor the endless phoning, nor even the crying of the babies who, overwhelmed by everything around them, are at the end of their tether.

It's the mothers' open display of entitlement, having to have everything at once, that exhausts me and reminds me too much of myself.

When Sonja was small there was barely anything I denied myself because of her. I took her everywhere, even to the cinema and of course to every restaurant. I adapted her to fit my life rather than the other way round. Occasionally I felt the desire to retreat, to restrict myself to one task – family, child – but this intention felt like a relic from the dawn of time which had overwintered in me and to which I should allow no breathing space. When I went back to my job as a curator after nine months and Richard stayed at home with Sonja for another three months, I thought we were a very modern couple. Richard said, "No, Linda, we've just swapped roles. The main breadwinner works, the one who earns less stays with the child. What's modern about that?"

The mothers in the cafés remind me of all this, and there's hardly anything I want to be less reminded about.

5

Finally it's autumn. The afternoon sun no longer climbs over the roofs to make it into the courtyards. They're in the shade all day long now. Only in Natascha's garden is there late light. On my last day of chores, before I turn off the water and leave the garden to its winter sleep, I meet the new tenants of the next-door plot. The woman parks her bike, unlocks the gate and enters her new realm with resolute footsteps. Her confident presence makes her look deceptively tall, even though she's substantially shorter than me. She hasn't seen me yet; she has eyes only for the wilderness that needs to be tamed. But the husband spots me. He stays right behind the gate, stares over at me, looks at her, then back at me. He says my name in disbelief, almost reproachfully, and the woman understands.

Recovering from the shock, Richard comes up to the fence and says, "What are you doing here?"

"I could ask you the same," I reply, adding quickly, "I'm helping a friend who's away for a while."

Brida Lichtblau offers me her hand over the fence. Her grip is firm.

"Hey, it's great to meet you," she says.

"Why didn't you say anything?" As ever when Richard feels uncomfortable, he pulls his shoulders up slightly and bobs up and down on the balls of his feet.

"I couldn't have guessed that you'd have a plot too. You used to find people who had allotments so strait-laced."

"Oh, really?" Brida purses her lips and narrows her eyes.

"Richard didn't want to spend his afternoons and weekends doing up a cabin and having an early-evening beer," I explain.

"The landlord is putting parking spaces in our courtyard, so we can't sit out there anymore," he says in justification.

"You don't need to justify yourself," I say.

There's something very natural about the way they are together, something I hadn't expected. Next to her Richard is a man rather than a heap of misery. Someone who's life is visible in his demeanour, but who stands tall and feels joy. Someone whose grey hair is neatly cut, who isn't letting himself go and whose gaze goes in the same direction as that of the woman he's now beside. A thought automatically shoots through my head: it's not our love that went astray, merely our common outlook.

When they've left my energy deserts me; the way home feels endless. I didn't know what effect the real thing would have as opposed to the abstract idea. Seeing him and her together was different from merely knowing about them. Like in a maelstrom, everything is now spiralling downwards, and however soundly I build my structure out of work and routine during the day, the nights pull it down. Every night is a chasm through which I'm squeezed and thrown back out into the world the following morning. When I wake up I sometimes look for Sonja, and often for Kaja too, and when the realisation dawns the day lies before me like endless expanses, like deserts or oceans or mountains, their peaks veiled with clouds. I yank open the window, gasp for air and ask myself again and again: Why another day?

The appointment with the notary is on a gloriously bright November's day. Richard turns up late, gives me a curt greeting and hurriedly holds the door open for me. An hour later it's official: the flat is going to the new owners for 785,000 euros. Richard is getting a third of the proceeds and I will have two-thirds. He could have insisted on half, but is content to take the smaller share because when we purchased the flat only a third of the capital we put in was his.

Afterwards we wander through our old neighbourhood, past the funeral directors with its pretty display – small wooden crates in staggered piles with miniature scenes of the most varied types of funerals and, beside these, urns that look like home accessories, watched over by individual hanging origami angels. The boss is in the window. Recognising us, he raises his hand in greeting. We greet him in return and go on to the corner café where Richard, Sonja and I began dozens of our Sundays. The breakfast here is wonderful, there's no Wi-Fi and no annoying music.

I order the dish of the day and a quince spritzer, Richard a double espresso.

For the first time today he looks me in the eye.

"I hope we've done the right thing."

I shrug with a smile, but he doesn't return it.

"I went back to the flat last week. All the art is now at the studio. You must come and tell me what you want."

"The Klinger Cassandra, the Claudia Berg prints, the Gerhard Altenbourg watercolour," I say. "Two or three pictures from your woodland cycle and your big portrait of Sonja."

He hesitates before answering. "That's fine. I'll bring them over." He nods a few more times. "Sometimes I get the feeling that none of this happened," he says softly, "and that Sonja didn't—"

I shake my head and he falls silent. Nothing can dispel the awkwardness between us. Apart from Sonja there's nobody

I've ever been closer to than him. And yet such closeness can become distance again.

"How are things with Brida?"

The surprised look on his face is followed by a lengthy pause.

"Not always easy," he says eventually. "Undine doesn't particularly like me, which is mutual, by the way. I make an effort, of course – I am the grown-up after all, but she's just impossible. Moody, lazy, always spoiling for a fight."

The drinks are put on the table in front of us.

"She's in her last year at school, having switched after Year 11 and repeated Year 12 because she was absent so often. She wants to spend a year abroad next autumn. Estonia. I hope she doesn't back out."

Sonja never wanted that, I think. She never wanted to leave Leipzig, go away from her parents, siblings and friends. She was a deeply rooted plant and an anxious one at that.

"Why's she so difficult?" I ask.

With a shrug, he says, "Who knows? To be honest I've no desire to engage with it. But I suspect it's connected with the fact that Hermine, Brida's elder daughter, moved down south to live with her father when she was fourteen. Undine's hardly seen her since, and the relationship between Brida and her ex is riven with conflict. All that patchwork shit.

"Anyway," he continues, "next month I'm moving into a new studio, and I'll also be able to sleep there. That will ease the situation. It's in Eutritzsch, high up and light with a view of the railway tracks. Really beautiful. You must come by sometime."

"I will."

Then my food is served. I eat quickly and without much relish. When I see Richard stealing a glance at his phone a second time, I signal to the waiter for the bill.

I walk back, past the funeral directors where the lower part of a new, light wooden coffin is being carried out and loaded onto a dark-blue Sprinter with tinted windows. It doesn't look like a hearse. The old estate cars with curtains used to remind us subtly of our mortality as they drove past, whereas with modern Sprinters you imagine a transport of furniture.

Putting one foot in front of the other I return to my car and drive to my street, my block. I go up the stairs to my flat and close the door behind me.

The sun is setting, night is falling and I take two pills to rescue me. The sun comes up again and I'm still here. I sit out my time, watching from my place on the sidelines how simply everything goes on.

I get regular texts from Natascha, pictures and videos of farm life in southern Germany. Nina is always smiling; she seems to be well, but Natascha says she's still not doing the minimum amount of work required for her to be allowed to stay there. Without someone helping her all the time she would do nothing apart from sing and sit amongst the animals. Her disability is too severe, Natascha writes, and besides, the whole thing is a pretty closed institution, unlike what it says in the advertisements. The disabled people live in complete isolation from the world of "normal" people. Young volunteers look after her, but are clueless as to all that this entails, and when they've finally got their heads around it they leave. New, clueless volunteers then arrive, who've been given the opportunity to try their hand out on the disabled residents, to prove to the world and their parents what good people they are. Her message finishes with an angry emoji and a crying one. I don't know how to reply. I'm ashamed. Sitting on half a million euros I'm waiting for death, while Natascha is fighting for herself and her daughter.

6

At the end of November two messages haul me out of the lethargy of the shortening days. One is from Natascha, announcing in a few words her and Nina's definitive return to Leipzig. The second is from my mother, declaring her intention to visit me on the first weekend of Advent. Both arrive on the same day, two hours apart.

I answer Natascha immediately, but let my mother wait. I don't mean to torment her, I just don't know how to respond. The most honest answer would be to say no without giving any reasons. *Dear Mama, I'm afraid that weekend doesn't work for me.* But I wouldn't put it past her to turn up anyway, stand with her small, expensive wheelie suitcase outside the door and keep her finger on the bell, ringing the neighbours' bells too, if necessary. Now that she's finally taken the decision to visit her daughter, nothing apart from illness or death will hold her back. *Dear Mama, I'll book you a hotel nearby. I don't have a spare bed yet. Let me know what train you'll be on and I'll pick you up from the station. Love, Linda.*

I can't bring myself to express any pleasure at the prospect of her visit into my message, but I don't suppose she'll notice the omission.

As ever when some incident undermines the monotony of my days, I take a higher dose of sedatives to circumvent the risk of my anxiety escalating into panic. About twenty minutes later I reliably fall asleep with the last thought of the day, which is to replenish my stock of medicine.

Over the last few years little has changed in Dr Judith Gabriel's surgery. The horse pictures on the walls of the waiting room have gone, replaced by typical surgery art – abstract experiments with colours, nice to look at but not particularly thrilling.

My former doctor recognises me at once. She leans across the table slightly, resting her forearms on it, and says, "I've often thought about you. How are things?" I give her a brief summary of the last few years, mentioning the doctor in the small town who was always willing to write me prescriptions. She hasn't heard of him. Dr Gabriel wants to know if I've been attending cancer aftercare, had other screenings, whether I'd like a skin check, a full blood screening test, a general consultation. For example we could see whether my iron levels are OK, my vitamin D level, my B vitamins, and the hormone levels need to be checked too, the dose adjusted if necessary. She speaks quickly, clearly, emphatically and I say, "I need sleeping pills, that's all."

A brief silence follows a tiny shift in her facial expression.

"You know it yourself but I have to tell you again: at least one of the medications you're taking has already led to a physical and psychological dependency. Together we ought to find a way to help you out of this."

"I really appreciate your efforts, but thanks, no."

My gaze falls on her screensaver – spectacular photographs of the natural world alternate with churches, fountains, all kinds of monuments and lots of pictures of a horse standing, trotting, galloping, rolling on the ground or lying in a green pasture.

"May I ask why you don't want any screenings?"

I don't hear any reproach in her voice, just objective interest.

"Screenings are the protective wall against death," I say, looking her in the eye. "We put it off for as long as we possibly can. And what do we gain? Time. Pure time. But time in itself has no value unless it's filled with meaning."

Dr Gabriel does not avoid my gaze. Her face remains unmoved.

"Modern medicine is a reflection of society," I continue. "Today, life is primarily measured in quantity, detached from meaning, form, happiness. Almost every medical intervention is designed to prolong life. But why?"

I'm surprised by myself and not even sure that I believe what I'm saying. But Dr Gabriel seems to be taking me seriously.

"Interesting," she says. "You ought to tell this to my patients in their eighties who sit here every day demanding that I rid them of all their minor ailments. I'm a doctor, not a magician. But let's stick with you. Is there really no point to your life?"

"Not at present."

"Not at present," she repeats, with emphasis on the *at present*. "Your daughter's death," she adds, saying it more to herself than to me.

"You remember."

"Of course. I've often wondered how you are."

"Hmm," I say.

"You're not my only patient to have lost a child."

"Do you have children?" I ask.

"No," she replies. "I didn't want any, either. But I do have a godchild and a horse, and I'm fully stretched with them."

Her eyes briefly wander to the pile of index cards, then to the watch beside the computer.

"What about if we just checked your TSH level?" she says, pivoting back to medical matters. "The right dose of thyroxine makes a big difference. How many micrograms are you on?"

"One hundred and twenty-five."

"There's scope to increase this."

We agree that I'll have a blood test and she'll call me if my dose needs to be changed.

In the waiting room the receptionist hands me a prescription for the sleeping pills. Her sour expression tells me what she's thinking. I thank her kindly and smile broadly into her disapproval. I don't care what she thinks so long as I get what I want. The little blue slips are stowed in my bag, and being in possession of them immediately calms me.

Natascha's first message after her return is a photo of the garden with an astonished-face emoji and the words: *Thanks so much!!! You've clearly got too much time on your hands.*

We meet the following morning at her flat, which is on the ground floor of a cheaply renovated period building. It's a cold, dry day; unpleasant gusts throw dirt into the air. Packaging spills from almost all the public dustbins and is tossed about by the wind. Crows peck at leftovers, use their beaks to pull pizza boxes from the bins and then work at them until the tasty morsels are freed. A gust blows something into my right eye. I steer to the edge of the bike lane and try to wipe it out, but it's deep beneath the upper lid. My eye is watering, and when I'm finally outside Natascha's block I can barely open it.

Her flat is dark. Now, in late autumn, when there are no leaves left on the trees, it's at its lightest, she says. In summer she has to switch on the lights during the day. I'd always imagined Natascha's flat to be vibrant and a jumble of new and old furniture, colourful cushions and throws, lots of odds and ends, incense sticks everywhere. Instead I enter plain white rooms with furniture that looks almost unwelcoming. There are no shelves. Everything is stored in cupboards with smooth fronts.

"Whatever Nina finds she puts in her mouth," Natascha tells me. "We've been to A & E a few times, because she had buttons, coins and other stuff stuck in her throat. That's why it looks like it does in here."

She's lost weight. In the colourful layers of clothing that usually give her a wild appearance and a *joie de vivre*, she now looks like someone who's struggling to make ends meet and so is wearing an old aunt's outsized things. The colours and shapes clash with the person who greets me.

Nina prances around us, singing, then goes off again to her bedroom, which is full of chains of lights up high. A diffuser puffs out steam that smells of bergamot. I recognise the melody of an aria, without being able to say which opera it comes from.

"She's in a Mozart phase at the moment." Natascha shrugs as if to say there's nothing she can do, and invites me into the kitchen. We drink bitter green tea from crude ceramic bowls and she asks, "What's up with your eye?"

"Oh, something just flew into it," I say dismissively. "It'll wash out."

She nods faintly, then looks at me and says, without any discernible connection, "This morning I opened the Bible at a random page and read the first verse that caught my eye: 'He delivereth the poor in his affliction, and openeth their ears in oppression.' From the Book of Job."

Staring vacantly past me, she says in a flat voice that now she's got to stay at home with Nina and can't work again until a place in a daycare group becomes free. She can't say how long that's going to be – definitely months, maybe years.

"How about having her looked after at home?"

She gives a bitter laugh. "Do you have any idea what that costs? I don't have any money, Linda! I'm broke."

She sweeps her hair back hectically. On her face is a forceful expression of defiance.

I know how Natascha feels. I can see her keeping up the façade with the last of her strength. Any unconsidered expression of kindness will make her collapse. I spare her phrases such as "If there's anything I can do for you" or "I'd really like to help".

Instead I say succinctly, "I'll cover the care costs for a year. By then you're bound to have found a solution." The words come out of thin air, but there's not a hint of doubt in my voice, and even as I'm speaking I can sense something shifting inside me. My body feels lighter, my mind clearer.

Something happens inside Natascha too. Her face changes, the tiredness abates for a moment, her muscles tense and her face looks receptive. I can see the idea unfurling and opening closed doors. Natascha smiles for a second, but at once she gives a vigorous shake of the head and taps her forehead.

"Impossible. I could never pay you back. I can't accept something like that."

"Why not? I don't want the money back. If I give it to you it's as a present."

Her eyes narrow to wary slits. "Should I be worried? Are you planning your exit?"

"I'd hardly announce it in such a brash way."

"That's true."

She sighs, closes her eyes and massages her temples.

My eye is now hurting so much that I'm beginning to sweat. I lift the upper lid for some relief.

"This is how we'll do it," I say. "You start looking, and when you've found somebody you give me a call."

Before she can raise any further objections I point to my eye, explain I've got to see the ophthalmologist, say goodbye, quickly grab my coat and bag, and make her promise to start looking for a suitable carer straightaway. Natascha nods hesitantly and accompanies me to the door. As we pass Nina's room I stop briefly. I recognise the birdcatcher's aria from *The Magic Flute*. The girl is sitting on the broad windowsill, gazing outside, and she keeps starting from the beginning of the song.

"Bye, Nina!" I call out. She turns to me, smiles, and I take Natascha's arm. "Don't worry too much. You've got a great daughter and there's a way. There's always a way."

I sit in the ophthalmologist's waiting room for almost three hours. My thoughts narrow by the minute until all they consist of are my eye, the pain, the treatment and the possible consequences. Just before I'm called, I'm not thinking anything at all. The pain rules. I want to be rid of it. That's all.

A few anaesthetic drops, an extremely confident and skilful pinch of the upper lid, which is now pulled up, a cotton-wool bud that runs across my cornea and takes a splinter with it. All in all it takes less than two minutes and the pain which had dominated everything is gone. I thank the doctor profusely, which earns me a puzzled look. I cycle back to my flat as fast as I can and sense a sudden energy that I don't want to let pass untapped. Once home I check my finances. I decide I'm going to keep only two-thirds of the half million euros. Enough to live off for a while; too little never to have to work again. I'll have to find a job, return to the rhythm of gainful employment and free time, and get close to the lives of other people again. The remaining third I'll divide into two portions: care money for Nina and donations to charitable causes. I can hardly wait to get rid of it. I'm absolutely certain that I'm doing the right thing.

7

I ask Natascha almost every day if she's found a carer. I spend hours at the computer, finding out about the possible donations I can make. After an appointment with an expert on aid that has proven to be effective I draw up a list and, in the days that follow, begin transferring money. With every sum that disappears from my account I feel lighter. My first donations are to deworming programmes in various countries in central Africa, as well as malaria prevention in children and projects run by The Humane League, an organisation dedicated to improving how livestock is kept. In my own city I give 7,777 euros each to the food bank, the children's hospice, the Nature and Biodiversity Conservation Union and the mobile disability assistance service. Seven is a good number, a primary number. Our life passes in seven-year periods, there are seven virtues, seven sins, seven sacraments, seven chakras, seven Wonders of the World, seven days of the week and seven visible planets. The menorah has seven branches and Rome was built on seven hills. I'm currently in the seventh cycle of the seven-year periods – in an age between forty-two and forty-nine.

With every one of these donations, each time I type the number into the digital transfer form, my strength gradually returns. Time is moving again and the only person I'd like to share these moments with is Richard.

Otherwise I keep living as I have been; I'm antisocial, almost invisible. I go out when it rains, snows and is stormy, and go into hiding when the sun shines. Even now I find work to do on the allotment, preferably in the morning and when the weather's bad. Sometimes I'm the only person on the entire site, which comprises over one hundred plots; I can tell this by the fact that the main gate is still locked when I arrive. I don't care about getting filthy and wet, and having dirt under my fingernails. My social contacts are restricted to Richard, Natascha, Nina and the occasional conversation in the stairwell with the dog man or the elderly couple from the flat next to mine. Every afternoon or in the early evening they put the papers they've read by my door. They have subscriptions for a regional and national newspaper, and they highlight with a marker the headlines of articles they think are important. This way I find out about their views very quickly.

Sometimes they open their door at the very moment I'm peering outside mine to see whether the paper's already there. We'll get into conversation and one day the woman tells me she used to have a child.

"He died, half a century ago," she says. "But you never get over it."

"Can you feel happy again?" I ask her.

"Yes," she says after a long pause. "But it's a different type of happiness. How should I put it? It has depth but no lightness."

She hands me the paper, turns and goes back into her flat, which I've only had brief glimpses into up till now. I like what I've seen. A wall of books and a wall of art, colourful rugs on the worn parquet floor and always this faint aroma of lemon balm. That's probably what it looks like and smells like, this other kind of happiness.

On Eternity Sunday Sonja has my undivided attention. In the basket of the white bicycle I place a large grave candle, which apparently burns for up to seven days. Somebody has already fixed an LED light to the frame, and hanging from the handlebars is a varnished wooden angel.

Richard is crouching by the grave when I arrive. My gaze alights on the gaudy bunch of flowers. He sighs. "You know who those are from."

"Him, presumably," I reply unmoved.

"How does he know where her grave is?"

"We made an official announcement of the funeral. He will have been standing somewhere, watching."

I crouch beside him and light another seven-day candle here too.

"Do you think it's really going to burn that long?" I ask Richard.

"We'll check. See you back here in a week?"

"Alright."

"Any plans for today?" I ask him as we stroll to the exit.

"Brida's got a reading in Dresden. I'm going along and we're spending the night there."

I see him with this radiant woman who needs a lot of light, a lot of attention and for whose sake he's even prepared to spend his free time on an allotment. I've been keeping tabs on her, reading everything there is to be found about her on the internet, hesitantly at first then purposefully. Her website is professionally designed and the information on it permanently updated. Brida Lichtblau uses social media, has a fan community amongst book bloggers and serves the needs of her readers via the most varied channels. She publicised her most recent crime novel with enticing excerpts. "The perfect holiday read", it says in *Brigitte*. "Challenging without being demanding", is the opinion of *Freundin*. And the *Frankfurter Allgemeine Zeitung* praises her "psychological sophistication, paired with a fast-paced plot".

I'd love to ask him who she really is, what hurts her, where she gets the strength to stand so upright, and how it feels to be famous. I'd like to get to know her. I've often found women more interesting than men. In conversation with women I've never been demoted to a silent listener. Sometimes I wonder what it would be like if all the women in the world came together to form one great force and changed all the existing rules. Would the madness about growth stop? Would there be less superfluous technology? Less rubbish? Less violence? My thoughts leap to the robotic lawn-mowers out in the village; women would never build robotic mowers, I'm certain of that. Another leap takes me back to Richard and the beginning of our relationship, when he said that women aped male behaviour rather than making the world more feminine. All of this goes through my head as we take the short walk together to the cemetery gate. But as we part company I just say, "Have a nice evening. And drive carefully."

Richard gives me a kiss on the cheek. His lips are dry and chapped from the cold. He puts on the lambswool-lined leather gloves I once gave him, gets onto his bike and pedals away.

8

On the first weekend of Advent my mother visits me as promised. She arrives at the main station early on Friday afternoon, gets out of the first-class compartment, waves and wheels her small expensive suitcase in my direction. We approach each other, me slightly more slowly. She's wearing dark trousers, a beige coat and a large scarf, presumably made of the finest cashmere. She hasn't aged one bit since I last saw her. Her thin skin sits taut and shiny over the bones of her face, she's carefully applied make-up to her eyes without lashes, her poise is excellent for somebody about to be seventy and there's a spring in her step. Life without a husband seems to be good for her. Since Konrad's death there's no doubt that she's blossomed.

After an unsuccessful kiss on the cheek in which our noses collide, she walks at a lively pace beside me to the tram stop, and I sense no more of that suppressed aggression characteristic of her when I was young. Without any discussion, she gradually submitted, yielded to Konrad's authority, a result of the combination of man, money and status. Evidently that is now over. Some deaths destroy those left behind, others release them. I don't dare articulate this; in any case, my mother would deny it. The affirmation of her profound grief over the death of her husband is part of the spectacle of her life.

On the tram she peers out of the window – wide-eyed and mouth slightly open – and all of a sudden I can imagine what she was like as a young woman. I think of Kaja's vet, who my mother knew when she was young, and I talk about her.

"Oh!" my mother says. "Renate Schaller. I remember her. Nice girl, dreadful parents. The mother was an alcoholic, the father a party secretary, one of the true believers. Is she still working, at her age? Poor thing."

She shakes her head and looks out of the window once more, the subject now seemingly having been ticked off. Before this opportunity, like so many, goes to waste too, I ask her the question from which all others stem: "Why did you leave everything behind back then?"

She looks at me in surprise. She blinks, clears her throat and runs the tip of her tongue along her painted lips. I can see the workings inside her head, the pondering, the search for the right words, the defusing of the explosive force of my question. Then she takes a deep breath, holds it and exhales slowly, as she always does when having a stab at the truth. I feel completely alert.

"I was afraid, Linda. Some people hide when they're afraid, others run away. I ran. I mean, everything was falling apart here. I didn't have a husband, no work, no parents. I was all alone. If someone like Konrad wants me, I thought, then I have to snap him up."

"But you didn't even ask me. You just took the decision."

"You wouldn't have wanted to move away," she says indignantly. "Why should I have asked you? A thirteen-year-old!"

"Do you know that I never made another close friend? Never again, Mama."

"Oh, don't give me that now. You got the best education, you always had enough money, great hobbies, wonderful holidays, a family. Yes, Linda, a family. Konrad liked you even though you weren't his biological daughter."

"I know that. And I'm not blaming him for anything."

"I see! But you're blaming me!" Her eyes dart around frantically. "Don't we have to get off soon?"

"One more stop," I say calmly.

As ever when her conscience is stirred, she launches into activity. She starts rummaging in her handbag, buttoning up her coat, rearranging her scarf, adjusting her hair and pushing past me to the exit. I smile serenely. This time she's not going to escape. She's in a trap, just like I am, because we're going to spend the next two days together in my flat. What she doesn't yet know is that I haven't booked a hotel; she's going to sleep in my bed.

Reluctantly she lets me take her case and walks alongside me. We turn into my street and she looks at the light-coloured façades of the period buildings. An entire street of houses at least one hundred years old. Not those great, imposing late-nineteenth-century buildings; these are plainer, shorter, with smaller courtyards and no stucco on the ceilings.

"Do you know what Konrad always said when we were in the East?"

"When were you ever in the East?" I ask her, but she ignores me.

"'We paid for all of this,' he said." She gives a high-pitched laugh, then another.

"I hope you disagreed with him."

"What good would that have done?"

"Here we are," I say, when we're outside my block.

"Oh! I thought you were going to take me to the hotel first so I could get rid of my case."

"No, there's enough space in my flat."

Another "Oh" and a wary look, then my mother falls silent. In the worst-case scenario I've just triggered one of her dreadful migraine attacks and I won't be able to speak to her again until tomorrow. If I'm lucky, we'll talk. I open the door, pull her case into the hallway and carry it up the stairs.

As soon as we're sitting in my kitchen a storm rages outside and my mother starts talking about the weather. I let her talk; I know how the conversation will go. Very soon she'll complain that I never get in touch with my brothers, and I'll explain to her why that's the case. We don't have a connection, purely and simply because they were born when I was almost an adult, and still small children when I moved out. They're virtual strangers and unlike me in every respect. We don't have the same interests, values or lifestyle. I just don't know what I could talk to them about. They didn't even come to Sonja's funeral. They and their wives politely sent their condolences by phone and letter, and we haven't been in touch since.

Following the topic of my brothers will come the topic of Richard, then the lecture about pulling oneself together, gritting one's teeth and carrying on.

But today my mother seems to be somewhere else, not here at the table with me. I remember once when I was fifteen or sixteen trying to talk to her about my loneliness. I didn't have any real friends, no group, no sense of belonging. Deeply miserable but obediently I went to school, did after-school sports and then came back home. My days were meticulously planned; Konrad and my mother had organised my life in a way that looked like care, even love, but woe betide me if I wasn't sufficiently grateful or I didn't feel well. Only concrete physical complaints were accepted – high temperature, diarrhoea, vomiting. If it wasn't visible it didn't count. Especially not mental anguish. "I don't want to know," my mother would say, or, "You don't need to tell me that," or, "I'm not putting up with that too." Full stop.

She really didn't put up with it. Not *too*, and this *too* remained a mystery to me at the time. Now she's sitting opposite me, close enough to touch, and I'm just a few questions away from knowing the meaning of this *too*. What did you have to put up with at the time, Mama? What had worn you out so much that you had no energy or headspace for your uprooted daughter? I have to strike the right tone, eliminate the reproach from my voice. If I confront her, she'll clam up. We've never been so close as now, in this very moment. There was always somebody in the way, preventing the conversation. Konrad or Richard, my brothers or Sonja. Now the way is free, death has blasted it clear. The door to my mother's inner life is no longer locked. Gingerly I venture an attempt.

"What were they like for you, those first few years in Kronberg, I mean?"

My question brings her back into the here and now. "The first few years in Kronberg? They were good, of course. We were able to afford everything and your brothers were born. That was good, yes, those were good years," she says. She fiddles with the rings on her fingers, gold with expensive stones.

"But Konrad wasn't at all interested in your past."

"I don't think you can put it like that. He just had his own viewpoint."

"He turned everything into ridicule. Everything we said about the past! Sometimes he'd imitate you in such a despicable way that I felt physically sick."

"Oh, really? I don't remember that."

The wind whips rain against the windows and my mother whispers, "He was just disappointed."

"With what?"

Her right arm swings in a semicircle through the air as she says, "Anything and everything. With you, with me."

"Me?"

"You were so stubborn and yet he was so fond of you. Yes, stubborn. You'd come home and disappear to your room. You'd come down for supper and say nothing. He wanted to talk to you, but whenever he asked you something you looked at me when answering. I had to defend you all the time."

"I didn't notice any of that."

"Of course you didn't! That was the whole point. You weren't supposed to notice anything."

I learn why he was disappointed with her over the course of the evening, in which the degree of truth increases with the amount drunk. We began in the afternoon and my mother can take her drink. Unlike me she can drink without slurring her words, without sleeping badly afterwards or not at all. "You drink like a bloke," Konrad once told her.

Basically, Konrad's disappointment matched my mother's. If my brothers hadn't come so quickly, my mother says cheerily, helping herself to more red wine, the marriage wouldn't have lasted a year.

"I was a confident woman," she says, taking a large gulp. "I didn't need anyone to explain the world to me!"

Now it's late in the evening and the conversation has long since become a monologue. Interrupted by sighs, laughs, refills and gulps, I learn bit by bit the story of a woman who made a mistake and every year kept postponing the correction of this error, until it was far too late and Konrad eventually solved the problem by gassing himself in his car.

"He was such a know-it-all, he knew *everything* better than me! I knew nothing, he knew *everything*!"

She gives a wicked laugh; her sarcasm bores into my head. I've been on the water for a while by the time my mother empties the rest of the third wine bottle into her glass and her features threaten to derail. Now that the spring is gushing all I have to do is listen in silence, without disturbing the flow of her memories with questions or comments. I'm certain that there won't be any continuation tomorrow. The momentum of her honesty is happening now.

When my mother staggers into the bathroom shortly after midnight I'm wide awake. I'm not going to take my sleeping pills tonight. I order, understand, piece together and reassess. For a long time there was a gaping chasm between her words and my instinct, and even many years later I didn't trust my own feelings. At last I know how right I was, but at the same time realise that not everything was a lie. There were happy times, like our Italian holidays in large villas when my mother would already begin drinking moderately at lunchtime, and she and Konrad would often retire to the bedroom early in the afternoon for a *siesta*, while the boys were allowed to play Super Mario on the Nintendo and I roasted in the sun on a lounger by the pool, devouring one book after another. Konrad was generous. He liked making people happy, even though his generosity was focused on material things. He often brought *salame calabrese* from the Italian deli, fennel salami that I loved, and when I began developing an interest in art he made sure that I got to see every exhibition I wanted to see. But I also remember why I didn't like it when he asked me something. His questions were seldom open – they usually came with the right answer pre-installed – and an evaluation followed almost everything I said. He put his stamp on my experiences, and the stamp said "Nonsense!" or "Rubbish!" or "Waste of time!" Sometimes he'd also stamp what I said with a "Good!",

"Well done, Linda!", or "I knew it!" But his praise didn't feel any better than his criticism because the conversation finished there. After the topic was stamped it was ticked off and a new one was embarked on. There had been real dialogue with my mother, but since she'd become Konrad's wife, she'd conformed. After this evening I realise that her strength and courage had been insufficient to start all over again with three children.

After a whole hour in the bathroom, my mother is sitting as straight as a die at the kitchen table the following morning, drinking one coffee after another. The booze hasn't left any traces. She asks what the plans are for today and I offer her the ultimate tourist programme organised long ago: Christmas market, lunch in Auerbach's Cellar, motets at St Thomas's, cakes at Café Kandler, two hours of rest back here and then, in the evening, the Christmas Oratorio Parts I–III & VI at the Gewandhaus. I'm dreading the day; my mother is thrilled. She strides at my side in a shiny, lilac-coloured, quilted coat.

When we're in the queue outside the church Natascha calls.

"I've found someone for Nina!" she screams into my ear. "For nine months. A young woman who's stopped her teacher training and is looking for a job. She saw my ad in the city magazine. Just imagine, Linda, she plays piano and sings in a choir! Nina loves her already."

The news comes as such a relief that, shortly afterwards, when the high-pitched voices of the Thomanerchor ring out, I nod off on the hard pew beside my mother. It's only the pastor's sermon that jolts me back into the reality of the day, whose regimented schedule my mother is managing effortlessly.

Her mission seems to be complete. On Sunday morning, without having granted me another glimpse into the depths of her soul, my mother packs her suitcase and wheels it into the corridor. "Right, then!" she says, and I'm surprised to find myself wishing she'd stay longer. Her presence has been reassuring. My mother is with me, I'd thought during that sleepless night, feeling like a child that no longer needs to feel afraid.

But she does go and refuses point-blank to be accompanied. She doesn't like station goodbyes, nor tram ones. I'm only allowed as far as the door to the street; she turns one last time and waves.

Once she's left I head for the cemetery. The seven days since Eternity Sunday are almost up and, against probability, I'm hoping that the candle is still burning. I slow down as I walk the last few metres to the grave, my eyes half closed. I become obsessed by the idea that it is the flame of my life burning there – or not. It is hope that is extinguished there – or not. My heart thumping, I stake everything on this sign, and when I hear Richard say my name behind me, I open my eyes wide and take a look. It's still alight.

9

Christmas is looming. The closer it gets, the more I'm afraid of it. I should celebrate with them in Kronberg, my mother says on the phone; my brothers and their families will be there, but even as she's saying it she doesn't sound convinced. We both know I won't come.

On Christmas Eve I leave the flat early in the afternoon. On the pavement outside is the family from the attic flat with an elderly couple who I identify as the man's parents because of the striking resemblance. His wife is expecting another child, as is clear to see. So the little boy will be getting a sibling. He's brandishing a stick and making fighting noises, and it occurs to me that if you're a boy it must be a deeply rooted law to see a stick as a weapon. Sonja only ever saw a stick as a stick – sometimes, when she was on the beach on holiday, as a tool for writing your name in the sand – but never as a weapon. The boy holds the stick in both hands and lets it swish through the air.

"You can give me the stick now," his pregnant mother says, sounding irritated. He doesn't react. "Do you want to give me the stick, Valentin?" she says, now more strictly. No, Valentin doesn't want to and he won't either. If his mother and I were friends I'd tell her that a child that young can't understand a request disguised as a fake question.

I say a friendly hello and go on my way.

Shortly afterwards I tell Natascha about this. She laughs and says, "Poor boy!"

It smells of baked apples and scented candles, and a funny afternoon begins because Nina is squeaking with pleasure. As ever we don't have a clue what she's laughing about, but that doesn't matter. We laugh with her until we can't anymore. We stuff ourselves with delicious *Lebkuchen* and watch with broad smiles as Nina carefully spears her pieces with a fork before putting them in her mouth and chewing very thoughtfully. Natascha drinks *Glühwein* and thanks me over and over again for the money for Nina's carer. When it's dark, after we light the candles on the tree, she ceremoniously hands me three presents wrapped in gold paper: a thousand-page novel, a bottle of eggnog and tickets for the opera she's taking me to see. We allow the candles to burn down, get wrapped up and take a short stroll down the street to where around two hundred people have gathered outside a raised ground-floor flat. Musicians are standing in the open windows, introducing themselves and their instruments. The violinist at the middle window welcomes everybody, wishes us all a happy Christmas and gives the link where we can find the list and texts of the songs that we're now going to sing together. Everyone takes out their phone. Inside the flat lit by candlelight, the pianist plays the opening to "*Maria durch ein Dornwald ging*", then violin, viola, cello and double bass join in, one by one. We start singing, softly and restrained at first, but by the second verse we're more confident and sing at the tops of our voices. Nina, who until then has been flitting around nervously and letting out stressed, sharp cries, lifts her head, opens her eyes wide and is calm. In this inexperienced choir of total strangers I also give free rein to my voice and am surprised by its sound. By the time we sing the last song, "Silent Night", I'm not missing any notes and I don't fight the tears that run down my cheeks.

In the leaden time between Christmas and New Year, when my own stagnation is drowned out by the general stagnation, I unpack the last of the removal boxes. I hang pictures on the walls and find a suitable place on top of a tall, white-lacquered wooden chest of drawers for the bronze Cassandra bust that Richard and I bought at auction years ago. Her expression encompasses all the suffering of the prophetess who nobody believes. The daughter of the king of Troy foresees that the abduction of Helen will bring the Greeks to the walls of the city and that the wooden horse in which the warriors are concealed will seal Troy's destruction. Eventually she prophesies her own murder, without being able to do anything to prevent it. Being so impotent while knowing what was to come made her life horrendous.

I run my fingers over the smooth, cold bronze and think how good it was that I knew nothing. For seventeen whole years I had no idea that my happiness would end after these seventeen years.

Then I move the sofa to the middle of the room and drape over it the Christmas present from my mother – a merino-wool throw in mustard yellow and fluorescent pink. I clean the flat even though it's not dirty, adding essential oils to the mop water that disseminates their aroma into all the rooms. On the spur of the moment I drive to the DIY store and buy a peace lily, a philodendron and a large monstera, which soon frame my sofa. These little islands of beauty comfort me in the long hours of darkness, and the meaninglessness of my days gives way to a faint anticipation that as yet has no goal.

While cleaning and tidying up, I find Esther's letter. I read it again, word for word, and put the date of her wedding in the calendar that I've given myself for Christmas. It's the first entry for the coming year and, although I don't know if I'll go, it feels good to write something in.

In the past I would also add things to the calendar after the event. I'd write in spontaneous meet-ups, with precise details of the time, place and occasion, and of course I put everything that had to do with Sonja in the planner. All seventeen volumes are on my shelf, ordered by year and never opened again. This is the first calendar I've had since Sonja's death. There was nothing more to plan and even now I'm not sure whether plans become action. Three steps forwards and two steps back – ultimately, that's what it is. On bad days the other way around, even. I expect little of myself and am only seldom disappointed. In the past it was happiness that used to be special, now it's the absence of unhappiness: waking up, being without pain, being able to move, eat, breathe, walk, read, sleep. Thus the year draws to a close.

On the day before New Year's Eve I decide to visit Klaus and Bruni. It's a mild, slightly rainy day without the slightest chance of any sun, and the village welcomes me in all its touching ugliness.

"My goodness!" A smile unfurls on Klaus's round face, which grows increasingly broad.

Still by the gate he calls for Bruni, and I hear her answer in the distance.

"Well, well, well," she says when she sees me and starts to grin. "Who have we got here?"

"Let's go in," Klaus says, and Bruni rubs my arm affectionately. Klaus gives me a sideways glance. "I can't believe you're back! You look good, better than before."

"Yes, better than before," Bruni concurs.

Inside, the table is laden with coffee, schnapps, squirty cream, stollen, biscuits and *Lebkuchen*. I learn that Gunhild's daughter is taking drugs again and has left the village – without her child. Gunhild and her husband are now having to look after the old mother with dementia and their abandoned grandchild. Klaus says about the new neighbours – my replacements – that basically they're nice people, but they're letting the wood sorrel grow like I did and they don't have the foggiest about chickens. The woman who makes ceramics has been seen with another woman recently, and there was an "incident" in the home for disabled people. When I probe further, they exchange sombre glances.

"*That* kind of incident," Bruni says.

"The police were here," Klaus adds, his eyebrows raised.

"Who would fiddle with such a damaged person?" Bruni cries out angrily.

"People like that should be . . ." Klaus swishes his arm like a sword.

"They should," I concur.

"Everyone has their cross to bear," Bruni sighs.

"Some have several," Klaus says angrily, following this with an exasperated laugh and an anxious glance at his wife. Then Bruni talks about her breast cancer, now metastasised to her hip; there's little chance of a recovery. The breasts have gone, but now the bugger's in the hip, eating its way through there. But if she's lucky she's still got a few years left. Klaus says nothing, looking everywhere apart from at his wife. There are no tears, no complaints.

"A miracle," he cries. "We could do with a miracle, couldn't we, Boss?"

Bruni looks at him as a mother might her child. With a sigh she lays a hand on his shoulder.

"For heaven's sake, I'm not dead!" she says, seeing the awkwardness in our faces. "And if I'm still here in a year's time we'll get ourselves some alpacas. Klaus promised me that."

"Absolutely!" he says, now with the usual resolve in his voice. "If my boss wants alpacas, that's what she's going to get!"

For a few minutes I listen to everything that Bruni knows about alpacas, which is a lot. Her eyes widen. She talks about the animals as if she's been dealing with nothing else all her life. If you look an alpaca in the eye, she says, you fall in love at once. And if they spit, they don't do it more than a couple of times, because they get lockjaw which stops them from spitting anymore. She's also thought about the amount of pasture they need. The ceramicist's property comes with a piece of land that's three thousand square metres, most of it unused. The animals can live there.

When I enquire how much an alpaca costs, both of them shake their heads.

"Don't ask," Klaus says. "Too dear."

They've thought everything through. To acquire three animals, the pasture, shelter, vet fees and feed for the first year, they've budgeted ten to twelve thousand euros. I know at once that I'll contribute if it comes to it. The pleasure in their happiness would brighten my life. I was next door to the two of them for all that time without having any idea. I knew nothing of the cancer and nothing of Bruni's lifelong dream, nor did I have a clue about how important Bruni's happiness is to Klaus. I lived there blind, deaf and insensitive, without realising that behind the walls of the neighbouring house were the same struggles, fears, dreams and acts of love that happen everywhere. But now they need nothing short of a miracle, and when I leave I wish them exactly that. I say it like an incantation, several times in succession until they repeat it too and we're all muttering "a miracle, a miracle, a miracle" together. When I'm in the car and see them waving in my rearview mirror, I can't get the word out of my head. But it's not only "miracle"; the word is automatically joined by two others. "Miracle, mystery and authority." All of a sudden it dawns on me where I know these words from. I stop by the side of the road, put on my hazards and rummage in the cardboard box beneath the passenger's seat for the CD I gave Richard for Christmas a few years ago, which we listened to together so many times. The chapter entitled "The Grand Inquisitor" from Dostoevsky's *The Brothers Karamazov*. When Jesus, fifteen centuries after his crucifixion, reappears on earth in Spain at the time of the Inquisition, he's deemed an undesirable and is locked up. The grand inquisitor gives him a lecture about how people aren't strong enough to be free *and* happy as Jesus showed them.

"There are three powers, three powers alone, able to conquer and to hold captive for ever the conscience of these impotent rebels for their happiness – those forces are miracle, mystery and authority. Thou hast rejected all three and hast set the example for doing so."

Every time we heard it Richard and I were fascinated by this text. And while I listen to it yet again with undiminished enthusiasm, the words create a distance from my little life, raising me to a different level, into a realm of art to which the banal has no access.

"Oh, Thou didst know that Thy deed would be recorded in books, would be handed down to remote times and the utmost ends of the earth, and Thou didst hope that man, following Thee, would cling to God and not ask for a miracle. But Thou didst not know that when man rejects miracle he rejects God too; for man seeks not so much God as the miraculous. And as man cannot bear to be without the miraculous, he will create new miracles of his own for himself."

As I approach the city I imagine Richard sitting beside me. I miss him; I miss talking to him. As this absence spreads around my innards like a virus, I take the CD out of the player and chuck it onto the empty passenger seat. I drive the rest of the journey in silence.

On the morning of New Year's Eve I walk to the allotments. As I'd hoped I'm the only one there. It's too warm for the time of year. Wearing only a jumper I spend a while digging the weeds out of earth softened by the rain. I wrap a jute sack around the fig tree I planted in autumn to protect against the frosts that might come whenever, and cover the ground with coconut matting and three layers of bubble wrap that I fix with tent pegs from the cabin. I remember the Syrian man's fig tree that didn't survive the winter. I've swaddled mine like a freezing child, but I won't know for a few months whether that's good enough. I fill the bird boxes with peanuts and sunflower seeds, hang a dozen fat balls in the bushes, and the hours pass swiftly and acquiescently. Here on the allotments, time seems to be subject to other rules. An hour feels like a few minutes and half a day like an hour. As I work I get so hot that my cheeks begin to glow. My senses are sharpened, apparently unrelated thoughts come and go, and when I make my way home I feel a peace and satisfaction that carries me through the whole day and into the evening. Promptly before the deafening racket I take a double dose of pills and sleep through the change from one year to the next.

10

In January I venture out for the winter tour of the galleries at the Alte Baumwollspinnerei. In the past this was a much-anticipated fixture in the diary that I almost never missed. Today it takes all my courage. As ever, the visitors have spruced themselves up, forming a glittering contrast to the dark, cold and wet winter's day. Beautiful, well-dressed people are standing before the most recent artworks in the harsh light of the exhibition rooms. Many young people have come, their faces not yet worn or worldly-wise. Curiosity radiates from the youthful pairs of eyes and, in the midst of this relaxed, unpretentious seeing and being seen, I feel like I'm moving on thin ice. Out of the dozens of people I know from my time as a curator and head of the art foundation, nobody comes to talk to me. They all know and all of them cast fleeting, uncertain glances in my direction. *Is that her? Christ, she looks awful. She's really aged. A broken woman. Well, if you lose your only child . . . It's unimaginable . . .*

I can hear their thoughts and my instinctive reaction is to smile. The way they look, hesitate and offer no more than the hint of a greeting before moving swiftly on. What else can they do? This isn't the place for a deep discussion. What was I thinking of, coming here? I tour the galleries, stopping for a long while in front of a picture by Hans Aichinger who, like no other painter, captures adolescents in that difficult time between being a child and an adult, between anticipation and fear of the future. In each of his portraits I see my own daughter as she was when she died – the girl on the threshold of womanhood. As I become absorbed in this painting, I can see out of the corner of my eye a tall person approaching hesitantly. "Linda?" he says, part question, part statement. I turn to him.

I'm genuinely pleased to see Hauke again. It's been years since we last bumped into each other, shortly before I fled to the village. He's still Richard's best friend and sometimes Richard helps him out in the shop when the commissions are piling up and Hauke can't keep up, despite working overtime.

"Richard said you were back in town. How are you?"

His frank question comes as a relief and makes me give an honest answer.

"There are some good days now," I say. "Like today, for example."

I manage to ask about his children, both of whom have moved out. His daughter is studying psychology in Vienna and is always unhappily in love; his son has been doing a wood-carving apprenticeship since last autumn and he's had a steady girlfriend for two years.

"What about your wife?"

"My wife . . ." His gaze sinks to the polished concrete floor. "My wife . . . she's in the process of reinventing herself. No idea what place I have in all that." He shakes his head slowly, still lost in thought, then looks at me again and says, with a sarcastic undertone, "We can't hold on to anything, everything is in flux."

"What luck that you've got an expert right in front of you then," I respond. "I could give courses on not-being-able-to-hold-on."

The two of us laugh, and for a moment everything feels like it used to. Two acquaintances, seeing each other in a gallery, chatting, joking, laughing and admiring a picture together. All perfectly normal. And in truth it does feel normal. Out of sheer gratitude to Hauke for having approached me without embarrassment, I invite him for a coffee.

I can't resist asking him about Richard and Brida.

"You'd better ask him," he replies, but then, after a brief hesitation, he tells me it's a difficult relationship, not good for Richard's health but good for his art.

"Have you seen what he's working on?"

I shake my head.

"It's exciting. Quite different. No longer the hermetically sealed world of his earlier paintings."

"Do you think that's Brida's influence? Is she an inspiration?"

Hauke doesn't answer. His expression assumes an air of sympathy and I immediately swear that I'm not trying to interrogate him. In vain. He gives me a weary smile and reiterates that I'd be better off asking Richard myself.

"I understand where you're coming from," he says, "but I'm uncomfortable discussing their relationship. There's always tension, a lot of energy involved, if you know what I mean." His hands make a cut-off gesture in the air, like a conductor at the end of a concert. "Right, now I want to hear a bit about you."

Hesitantly at first, then with increasing fluency, I tell him about the last few years, the villagers, Kaja and the chickens, Natascha and Nina, and my intense loneliness on those bright summer's evenings. Hauke is a good listener: he doesn't judge and in the moments when I stop talking he waits for the silence to pass. When we say goodbye after almost two hours, it's as if I've been freed from a burden and I leave feeling pluckier and buoyed. On the way home I stop in the centre of town at the boutique where I used to buy too many clothes and leave soon afterwards with a moss-green alpaca-wool cardigan that I absolutely don't need.

February and March pass uneventfully. I divide my days up into small, manageable units of time that I fill with diverse tasks. In the garden I prune the apple trees when the moon is waning, as Gunhild taught me, and late in the afternoon I listen to readings of classics while trying out recipes from a cooking-for-one book. *The Magic Mountain*, *Doctor Faustus*, *Walks through Brandenburg* and *The Rider on the White Horse* keep me busy for around a hundred hours, not a minute of which I consider wasted. Step by step, almost without any emotional setbacks, I overcome the dark days, which I prefer in any case to the coming spring. In the flat I carefully cultivate my little oases of beauty. On an indigo porcelain plate there are always three fresh lemons, beside the Cassandra bust a single long-stemmed flower in a narrow vase – a red gerbera, yellow tulip or white amaryllis – colourful cushions and throws decorate the sofa, and I drink my tea from a Japanese cup with a filigree chrysanthemum pattern. The objects are not mere objects, they are balm to my wounded soul and bring me into harmony with the day.

In the mornings I've recently been doing a few exercises to dreadful but motivational music and I prescribe my social interactions like bitter medicine. I regularly meet up with Natascha and Richard, I see Hauke again, at the end of February I drive to Weimar for the day to visit Richard's parents, and in March I spend a week in Kronberg at my mother's.

Only seldom am I deluged by waves of grief and I know how to deal with them. If it happens in public I rapidly look for a quiet place, lean against a wall or sit on a bench and breathe. If it happens at home I throw myself into it and let myself be pulled under. At some point the wave spits me out again and for a few hours afterwards I feel absolutely nothing.

At the beginning of April it snows for two whole days. With the temperature hovering around zero the garden is dormant once more, punishing the impatient gardener. Anything that was put in the ground too early dies.

I'm drawn to the grave. Wrapped up warmly, I get onto my bike and struggle for a good half hour to the cemetery at the other end of town. It looks as if nobody's been here in a while. Dirt has gathered in the bronze magnolia blossom that decorates the marble stone. I brush the stone and the bronze, clean the inscription, sweep leaves to the side and plan the spring planting. In my hustle and bustle I don't feel the cold or any grief. I also stop by the white bicycle, remove the rubbish and am surprised by how habitual these tasks have become. They're now part of my life, just as Sonja was part of my life.

After the frost the temperature leaps to fifteen degrees and I begin planting the seedlings I germinated at home out in the allotment beds. A few weeks earlier I sowed the seeds in compostable grow pots, watered them, placed them on the windowsills and thought that having only one child is like sowing only a single seed in the soil, an idea that would never occur to any good gardener.

On one of the warmer April days I'm giving the cabin a spring clean. When I look out through the dirty window I see Richard on the neighbouring plot. He's wheelbarrowing several large bags of compost into the allotments, rose compost, hydrangea compost, raised-bed compost – all fertilised, incredibly expensive special composts. Brida isn't with him. One day when I wasn't here there was a major clear-up of her plot. Apart from the fruit trees and larger ornamental plants, everything has gone. The wilderness was ploughed and levelled.

Richard heaves the bags, one after the other, from the wheelbarrow and piles them up, then his gaze sweeps our plot. We're separated by no more than five metres and a cabin wall, but he can't see me. I resist the impulse to go out and call his name. My heart is beating fast and hard. He leaves the allotments with the wheelbarrow and returns soon afterwards with a new load. Twice more he fetches purchases from his car, which he'll have parked outside the main gate, then he leans the wheelbarrow vertically against the cabin and leaves without turning around.

On my way home I see everything as if beneath a magnifying glass. Scenes on the edge of my field of vision impose themselves: a father lifting his daughter onto his shoulder with a *hop-hop*; a pair of very young lovers entwined on a park bench, kissing; a group of teenage boys that remind me of rowdy chimpanzees; two young fathers carrying their babies in blankets, staring at their phones. I look up at the sky where the wind is tugging at a huge cloud and, a little later, scraps of cloud glide against the shining blue like hunks of candyfloss.

Then I see Freya. She's sitting on the arm of a bench, smoking with two other young women on some grass diagonally opposite Gohlis Palace. We greet each other with a discreet wave and now the other two look in my direction. As I continue on my way I mutter the words that Freya will be saying. "That was Sonja's mum, you know, my friend Sonja who was knocked down by the lorry." She'll condense our family's story in just a few words. Her pity washes behind me; I automatically walk more quickly. They don't yet realise how fragile their own lives are, how little weight their decisions will have in the face of those things that existed long before they did, and those that will simply happen to them. They have a small window of opportunity in which they break with their parents, cover their bodies in tattoos and scream their fuck yous at the world, or they consolidate their strength that remains unbroken and are able to do something constructive. I turn and our eyes meet. At a slight distance they look almost identical, so young, vulnerable and uniformed, with their short, straight fringes, oversized hoodies and baggy jeans, and tattered cloth bags covered in messages. They think they're individual, but they just want to belong somewhere. They don't know how lonely it is to be a true individual, a genuine solitary person.

At the allotment on the days that follow I look out for Richard, but he doesn't appear. Instead Brida turns up with two men in work clothes. They've arrived in a small van, bringing loads more plants – fast-growing, high-climbing varieties that will completely cover the fence to Natascha's plot this year and overgrow it. Brida gives the men, who I presume are from some horticultural and landscaping firm, precise instructions, motioning impatiently to them to go over there, then back here. Her diligence reminds me of my old self; I, too, was good at issuing orders with a gentle authority. Before she lets the men get on with the work themselves, she comes over to me.

"I just wanted to say a quick hello. I haven't got much time, I'm afraid."

"Doesn't matter," I reply. "We're bound to bump into each other quite often in the future."

She nods without the slightest change of expression. I'm sure she's not thrilled at the prospect of having to see Richard's ex-wife on a regular basis.

"Although," I add, with an eye on the plants beyond the fence, "if all of that grows up quickly . . ."

"We thought a bit of privacy would do us all good," she replies and I say, "Yes, probably."

The "we" pains me. Was making me invisible Richard and Brida's sole criterion when choosing their plants?

She looks away briefly, then says, "You've got to admit that this set-up isn't exactly ideal."

Her honesty surprises me. A good opener for a lengthy conversation. I could put on some coffee in the cabin and invite her in, but she's already glancing at her elegant watch.

"We'll get along," I say. "And, who knows? Maybe it'll give you some material for your next book."

"Possibly." She laughs as if she's been caught out. "Well . . . I take what I can get too. All writers do. We exploit our own lives as well as other people's."

"I'm excited to read your next book then."

She nods and a hint of uncertainty flashes across her face before she raises her hand in greeting and I have to force myself not to watch her go.

At the end of May, lilac, broom, peonies, poppies, daylilies, roses and all manner of flowers whose names I don't yet know are blooming in Natascha's garden. The Armenian poppy sends up thirteen large flowers. Dozens of insects dive greedily into the blooms, whose splendour lasts only a few days. Once I count four bumblebees, two honeybees and a large, blue-and-black carpenter bee on a single flower, competing for its nectar. With thick padding on their legs the bumblebees eventually stagger out first, as if drunk, and drone away sluggishly. I harvest kilos of rhubarb and use the leaves to mulch the young tomato, courgette, celery, cucumber and pepper plants. The work in the garden never ends, the cycle is perpetual, and in its infinity both reassuring and unsettling. It shows me how superfluous I am, and although this is something I've been under no illusion about, a more profound understanding of what it means leaves scars.

Natascha and I take turns at the allotment. We rarely see each other as I prefer to come at times when she's working. We leave each other messages in the cabin. *Please earth up the potatoes again*, she writes. *Don't forget to give the young apple tree plenty of water*, I write. Some days I can really notice how working in the warming sunshine gives me new energy. Then I pause and voice a quiet thanks.

On Richard and Brida's plot, paid helpers are undertaking a second major operation, making a pretty path out of rubble, constructing edges for beds and expertly planting more shrubs and bushes in galvanised wire-mesh baskets in the ground. While I spend half the day removing by hand the ermine moth caterpillars from our two old apple trees, I watch order taking shape next door. The caterpillars are hanging from the trees in their thousands, eating the leaves and abseiling on invisible threads. Their cocoons are sticky and dense; it takes me hours to pick them all off. By the time I'm done, the men in the neighbouring plot have finished their day's work too. They're standing on the path, leaning their arms against the fence and silently surveying the result. One of the two takes photos, which I imagine he's going to send to Brida. Then they pack up their stuff, reverse the van out of the narrow path towards the main gate and are gone. The next-door garden is now complete.

Later in the afternoons I go on long stomps out of town, on land where there are as few paths as possible so I can properly be alone. My desire to be in deserted places is always in inverse proportion to their frequency. I find them in some forests, some riversides, and on these walks I remember the strangest things. Such as that Saturday in my old life, when I went to buy a new loo brush and came home with a coffee machine. When Sonja and Freya endlessly baked cupcakes and sponges in Year 6, turning our kitchen into a battlefield at least once a week. When at the onset of puberty Sonja started calling us "Mum" and "Dad", using the English terms. When Richard asked me if it was alright if he painted Esther, because although he didn't like her that much, the back of her head was beautiful.

I don't hold on to these thoughts and images. They come and go, and the longer I walk, the more fleeting and the hazier they become. If I walk for long enough they are no more than colourful feelings that emerge inside, pass through me, are exhaled through the pores of my skin and get lost in the wind. I stop, raise my face to the sun or rain, and the contours of my body begin to flow, passing seamlessly into air and earth, and then I know: I'm here. I'm alive.

11

One Saturday in June there's a communal workday on the allotments. Natascha has asked me to stand in for her, and so at nine in the morning I'm outside the management office, waiting along with the others for the tasks to be allocated. I get given the job of weeding the path by the main gate. Equipped with a wheelbarrow, hoe and rake I set to work. I'd planned to listen to *The Stechlin* but then I see Richard standing beside me. He parks his bike, greets me with a brief hug and hurries on. Less than ten minutes later he's back with a pot of paint and a brush; his job is to paint the gate. And so we find ourselves side by side, my husband and I.

"If someone had told us ten years ago that we'd be in this situation we wouldn't have believed them." He shakes his head.

"Of course not," I say a touch too acidly, then ask if Brida's coming too.

"She had an almighty row with Undine and now she's in bed with a migraine." After a pause, he adds, "A real migraine with scintillating scotoma, you know, like your mother gets."

I nod and mention that my mother's migraines have disappeared since Konrad died. She told me this in passing when she came to visit in December and I drew my own conclusions.

Then I ask, "What's up with her daughter?"

"An eating disorder, she's already been in a psychiatric unit twice. She was actually doing better, but now it's all kicked off again and Brida flipped out. She accused Undine of being completely perverted if she was starving herself when the fridge is full."

"Did she really say that?"

"Brida's frightened, that's all. And when you're frightened you say bad things." He gives a tortured smile, then says, "How are you, Linda?"

"Not bad," I say. "In all honesty, not bad at all."

"Really?"

"Yes," I say. "Everything's different, but . . . I'm not bad."

Then I get weeding and he paints. Sometimes we exchange glances and smile. He paints, I weed, and all I want is for this to continue for a while. For us to work side by side and look at each other occasionally. He's the most important person in my life, even if nobody here knows it. While he carefully applies paint without making any splashes he tells me about problems at his school and other schools in the city, young boys calling their teachers whores and the fathers of these boys thinking that's OK. He talks about the high incidence of sickness, about burnouts and crying fits in the staffroom, final-year pupils who can barely string a decent sentence together, parents who expect the school to educate their children while allowing them unlimited screen time at home. But he also talks about the curiosity of some pupils, about aptitude, engagement and a fifteen-year-old girl who's always drawing, no matter what lesson she's in, and whose huge talent is almost scary, the way she handles her pencil with such ease, conjuring her comic worlds on paper. Then he switches consequentially to the deficits in education policy, to politics in general and world affairs.

"Oh, this world," is all I say.

"The world is out of its tiny mind," Richard says, taking a step back from the gate and checking the result of his efforts.

"Sometimes," I say, "I catch myself thinking about all the things Sonja was spared."

Richard puts an arm around my shoulder. "I'm going to the grave on Monday morning, around ten. Do you want to come?"

I nod, let my head sink onto his chest and stay like that for as long as seems decent, despite our separation.

On Sunday I put the roller blinds down because of the heat and don't leave the flat.

On Monday morning I treat myself to a sumptuous breakfast of fruit salad, croissant warmed in the oven, boiled egg and coffee with frothy milk.

On my way to the grave I see a new white bicycle. It's bare, the paint gleaming, still fresh. No clue as to the person who died here. I take out my smartphone, then enter the names of the streets that intersect here and the words *fatal accident* into the search engine.

Mother of three, thirty-seven, on her way home from work, mown down by a lorry turning right.

The traffic roars by regardless, pedestrians march on indifferently and cyclists whizz past without stopping. I go on too, after a check of the time and a message from Richard. *Are you still coming?* he writes. *Be there soon,* I reply.

Later, over lunch in the canteen of a theatre for children and young people, where we went many times with Sonja, I tell him about the woman who died.

"I'll have forgotten her by tomorrow," I say flatly.

"That's normal. You can't feel for everyone." When I am

silent he says, "There are lots of people who haven't forgotten Sonja."

And as if to prove it, he shares a memory.

"Do you remember," he says, "how her head always used to hurt because her ponytail was too tight?"

"But she wanted it that tight!"

He nods. "And in the evening she'd take out the tie and brush her hair backwards, mostly in the kitchen, which used to drive you mad!"

"Because her hair would end up in the food!" Then I add quickly, "And do you remember how there was a phase when she and all her friends would do that weird thing with their bodies . . ."

"You mean that *move.*"

"Exactly, that *move*, thrusting the hips forwards and backwards and doing the same with their bent arms."

His gaze turns inwards momentarily, then he starts to grin.

"And the microwave animal?"

"Oh God, yes!"

We were with all three children in a bookshop in town, and Arvid discovered these cherry stone pillows in the shape of animals. Ylvie, who often spent days in bed with stomach cramps and a lot of drama when she had her period, wanted to have one. Richard gave the OK and Ylvie chose a cat. Sonja, who couldn't have been older than five, looked at the animal. "That's a mic-ro-wave an-i-mal," Ylvie said. "You put it in the microwave, it gets hot and then you put it on your tummy." Sonja picked up a dog and said, "I want a mic-ro-wave animal too," but Richard immediately and firmly said "No", and because we'd agreed that we wouldn't question one another's decisions in front of the children, that was that. Sonja's voice sounded strained. "But I want a microwave animal too," she chuntered. We went down the stairs to the till. "I want a microwave animal too," she demanded, close to tears. At the till she started to sob. Then she took a deep breath: "Iwanta-microwaveanimaltooIwantamicrowaveanumaltooIwantamicro-waveanimaltooIwantamicrowaveanimaltoo." She shouted as loud as she could and threw herself on the floor.

"IWANTAMICROWAVEANIMALTOO!"

We'd never seen her like this before, and when the fit was over after a good quarter of an hour, which to me felt like an entire day, Richard carried her into the bike trailer, where she fell asleep a few minutes later.

Richard is still smiling. Then he shovels in a forkful of *spaghetti alla puttanesca* and looks at me expectantly.

"Once," I say, "she took one of Ylvie's children out in the pram on her own – Arne, if I remember rightly – saying, 'I hope people will think he's my baby.' She might have been fourteen at the time, but she didn't look any older than twelve."

"That's right!" Richard laughs heartily. "But do you remember, she called us while she was out. She didn't know what to do because the baby was screaming like mad. She was distraught."

"Oh . . . I'd totally forgotten that."

"You were hysterical. You gave her all kinds of suggestions over the phone, but none of them worked. The baby kept screaming. The only person who remained perfectly calm was Ylvie."

Having finished every last strand of pasta, he pushes his plate into the centre of the table and grins.

"And I hope you remember how we suddenly felt in love again when Sonja started seeing Niklas."

There was a buzz and tingling in the air, an effervescent giddiness that Richard and I got caught up in too. Sonja's delight was likewise our delight; we benefited from her being in love. The happiness in those days was tangible, and unlike the many occasions when we were only aware of such happiness when it was lost, this time we realised it in the moment. For a few unreal, wonderful weeks, the trajectory of Sonja's, Richard's and my life went upwards in sync, heading to its zenith, only to plummet.

"You wanted to sleep with me all the time," I say.

"Yes . . . sometimes we'd meet up between your classes, and remember that time we went to a hotel?"

In an exuberance of lust we ordered all kinds of things from a sex-toy company. The package, which gave no indication of its contents, arrived by post one day after Sonja's death. We never opened it.

"Where's the package?" I ask. "You didn't . . ."

"Oh God, no. It's not at Brida's. It's in the studio, still unopened."

Like pretty much everything, sexual desire was stifled by Sonja's death. Not even the news of one's own impending death kills lust as reliably as the death of a child.

Richard seems to be thinking along similar lines. His gaze is turned inwards, then he suddenly looks harried. He finishes his water in a single gulp and looks at the watch I gave him years ago. It has a midnight-blue face, silver hands and a dark-brown leather strap. The sort of thing that used to be passed down from generation to generation.

"Sorry, I've got to go," he says guiltily.

I wonder where and why. His embrace feels different from usual, firmer and more heartfelt, and when, on his bike, he turns to me I wave as cheerily as I can.

In the blistering early afternoon heat I cycle home, my mood now changed. I feel oppressed by the totality of the city's rubbish – the discarded plastic, broken bottles, pools of spilled alcohol brimming with flies, barbecue leftovers surrounded by crows, dog shit smeared everywhere, chewing gum trodden into the pavement, cigarette butts, spit, broken rental bikes and e-scooters ready for the scrap heap, even in the farthest corners of the city's woods, and the neglected, dry trees by the sides of the roads. Not to mention the people. Some aggressive, some loud, some apathetic in their fat bodies, heaving themselves forwards in clothes that are too tight or big and shapeless, their eyes staring at their phones. They arouse my sympathy and disgust at the same time. I don't want to see them, don't want to have to think about why they've given up their shape and dignity.

Back home I pull down the roller blinds to shut out the sun. We're in for some tropical nights with temperatures well over twenty degrees. Storms are predicted, the humidity will rise and a sticky heat will make its way into every corner of the flat. I stand in the darkened rooms and then it sweeps me away. I only ever wept for my child, not for Richard. Now I'd be prepared to go back to him. Until now he would have had to wait. I howl my despair at the walls and into the cushions, stand under a cold shower and stay there until I'm shivering and my teeth chatter. My longing for intimacy has been reawakened and this has softened me. I need to return to the cold chamber, which has prevented me from melting or dissolving. It's deep inside me, in a place where longing and suffering end.

12

For a few hot days in July I have to force myself to live.

With a kind of numb detachment I go about my daily routine, greet neighbours, supply my body with sufficient nutrition and liquid, and am surprised by how impeccably it's functioning. *Come on, get up, it's going to be fine,* I coax myself when I wake, *a cup of coffee, cold shower and you'll be ready to face the day.* I manage to harvest the berries on the allotment, deadhead the roses, tie in the tomato plants that have shot up, mulch some beds with fresh grass cuttings, take a few early-morning swims in Lake Kulkwitz and write my long-overdue letter to Esther, in which I tell her honestly and bluntly why I'm keeping my distance. I leave nothing out, not even the feeling – totally unfounded, I suspect – that she's taken advantage of my suffering and delighted in it. It's a monstrous thought, and to understand the effect my words are going to have I read the letter out loud, substituting my own name for Esther's. "Dear Linda", I begin, and when I get to the end and let the words resonate, the truth seems harsh but not unreasonable.

One morning my mother calls and tells me she's planning a big trip. She's found a "travel partner", she says, who she's going to tour the Baltic with for several weeks.

"A travel partner?" I ask in astonishment. "Yes," she says, "it just happened. Total surprise. I met him in the bookshop, you know that lovely one we have here in town?"

Then she tells me something inconsequential about the nice bookseller, I know the one, she says, "handsome", who's always got such good recommendations, who knows every customer back to front and knows what they need, as if he could tell just by looking at them what they want to read. While I let her clumsy attempt to say nothing about the "travel partner" pass without comment, it feels as if I'm the mother and she the child.

That same day Natascha calls and apologises for having left me alone with the allotment. The reason is her new job as a radio announcer. Finally more money, more security. But actually she wanted to ask if I'd like to accompany her and Nina to *Klassik airleben*.

We used to go every year, Richard, Sonja, myself, Ylvie, Arvid, and often Freya with her parents. It's as much a part of Leipzig's musical year as going to see the annual performances of the *Christmas Oratorio* and the *St Matthew Passion* or *St John Passion*. The two concerts given by the Gewandhaus Orchestra, which take place on successive nights, are the last of the season before the musicians' summer break. Around thirty thousand people sit on picnic blankets on the great meadow in the Rosental, bringing baskets of food and drinks, and listen to a pot-pourri of nice classical pieces.

"Next year, perhaps," I say.

"Life is happening *now*," she says.

"I can only tolerate people as individuals," I retort. "En masse they're too much for me."

"You can get up and leave whenever you want."

She won't give up and, feeling too feeble to say no, I agree.

On the morning of the concert the creases in the pillow have pressed so deeply into my face that the lines don't disappear until long after breakfast. I'm getting old, I think, unperturbed.

A couple of hours later I drive out to the village. I want to find out if the miracle has happened.

Klaus is standing outside with the blowtorch.

"Well, well," he says cheerily, then comes over and hugs me tightly. The moment he lets go I scan his eyes for a sign, but he looks away and points to the pavement outside my old house, where weeds are growing from every crack.

"They're no better than you," he says, shaking his head, then he beckons me in.

I sit on the bench by the front door while he goes inside to look for Bruni.

"The Boss is on her way," he calls from the hallway. And then she comes – thinner and wearing a colourful headscarf that exposes stubbly new hair.

"Stoning sour cherries," she says. "A bugger of a job."

She holds out her forearm by way of a greeting and I grab it with both hands like someone drowning. I don't dare ask how she is.

"The chemo was successful. No new metastases and the old ones have shrunk," she says tersely, then adds drily, "The weeds don't go."

An abstraction darts across Klaus's face, something I've never noticed in him before.

"I mean, I couldn't leave my Klaus on his own. He'd starve to death."

Bruni laughs and Klaus turns up the quivering corners of his mouth while tears roll down his cheeks. He turns away abruptly and stomps off. Bruni shakes her head, looking anxious.

"It's doing Klaus in," she says. "His heart is too soft."

She shrugs, at a loss, then we go into the kitchen, drink iced coffee with cream and stone the rest of the cherries together. On the dresser is a book with a grinning alpaca on the cover.

"We're going to visit the breeder next week," Bruni says ceremoniously. "To have a bit of a nose around."

She explains that you have to have a minimum of three.

"They're herd animals, they need their friends, otherwise they tussle with their owners and that's not fun."

Klaus reappears, picks up the alpaca book, sits with us and browses the pictures.

"They're such sweeties, those animals. When they're here you've got to come and meet them."

He gets up again, takes an iPad from the cupboard and goes to a website with alpacas for sale. This is the right moment for my offer. We look through the animals together, and when Bruni points excitedly at a breeding mare – white with brown patches behind the ears – for sale with colts for three thousand five hundred euros, I tell them I want to contribute. I say it as naturally as possible and though the two of them stare at me aghast, the protest I'd feared doesn't materialise.

"Are you serious?" Klaus says.

"Absolutely," I reply, adding, "I've been planning this ever since you first talked about them."

Bruni gives me a hug. She won't let go of me. A shudder courses through her body, but eventually she sits down and wipes her face with her apron. We settle on my being a sort of godparent. Klaus claps me on the shoulder and looks highly satisfied. When I leave Bruni gives me a freezer bag full of cherries, then I drive off, hooting my horn and feeling light of heart. While waiting for a gap in the heavy traffic I turn around. At that moment the two of them are briefly washed with light before the wind drives more clouds in front of the sun. But the radiant image has already imprinted itself on my mind as an acknowledgement of the miracle.

In the evening I'm tentatively excited as I make my way to the summer concert. With a bit of make-up – for the first time since Sonja's death – and dressed in a light-grey linen dress, I worm my way through the tightly packed crowd on the meadow. Richard looks twice in my direction then away again. Finally he recognises me. He and Brida are sitting with another couple on a multicoloured blanket. He stands up and comes over, while Brida keeps talking to the others. She gives me a fleeting glance.

"You look . . . different," Richard says as he embraces me.

"In a good way?"

"Fantastic. It's just so . . . unexpected." He shakes his head and laughs. "I'm talking myself into trouble here."

"You've got skinny," I say. He gives a dismissive shrug, then turns to Brida, who gets up very slowly and comes over to us in her typical poise – ramrod straight, head tilted back a fraction.

"I didn't recognise you," she says, sounding almost reproachful. "Nice dress," she adds. "Grey really suits you."

At that moment Natascha calls. "Spotted you," she says. "Look towards the stage, on the far left you'll see me waving."

"We're sitting over there," I tell Brida, pointing to Natascha who's waving her arms madly. "You can swing past if you like."

In my mind I add *you and my husband.*

When I get to Natascha she immediately pours me a small bistro glass of wine. A third of the bottle has already been drunk and Natascha's lips and teeth are stained a bluish-purple. I find her greeting over the top: kisses left, right and left again, followed by a tight hug which I want to free myself from at once. Her eyes are darting around frantically; everything about her behaviour seems extravagant and a touch overblown.

When the music begins Nina leaps up, lets out a cry of delight and flaps her arms. Her joy is immediate and free. People around us turn their heads; some stare uninhibitedly, others show their sympathy by quickly looking away again, embarrassed, while a few give us friendly smiles. Natascha says you need to keep your distance from the gawpers and the over-friendly ones. The former just aren't nice, whereas the latter are trying to display their moral superiority. The honest ones are those who turn away, because that's what people are like: they look when something unusual happens and look away again when caught in the act. Her compulsive rationalisation seems to me to be a ruse to avoid being hurt, but I don't contradict her. What's alien and different, she continues in a loud voice, has snapped people to attention since the dawn of time. It's genetic and ultimately no more than a protective reflex, because if what's different turns out to be a danger, you have to be ready for flight. At that moment Nina emits a drawn-out scream of excitement.

"Right," Natascha says, "now we've got their full attention."

Three pieces of music later Nina is still skipping with delight. A gust of wind sweeps over us and the first drops of rain fall. Some people begin packing up their stuff, others open large umbrellas, but the wind gradually turns into a storm. The orchestra plays against the rustling of the leaves in the surrounding woods and the thunder rumbling in the distance. But then thousands of people decamp at once. In the turmoil Richard looks for me at exactly the same time that I'm trying to spot his face. Smiling, he raises his hand and remains in this pose for a moment. Only when the rain starts pelting down, drenching us in seconds, does he turn away.

Natascha seems to have sobered up at a stroke. She has to drag Nina, who doesn't want to leave; she struggles and begins to scream. I push her forwards while Natascha pulls her. A defiant body is difficult to move, even one as delicate and light as Nina's.

When we get to the car the sky is already brightening again. Despite what she's drunk, Natascha insists on driving, and when I ask if there's any cause for concern she shakes her head. "It's just been a fuck-awful day," she says.

"Shall I come with you?"

"No, absolutely not!" she says.

When she sees the look of doubt on my face Natascha assures me that she's not going to drink any more when she gets home, she's going to go to bed, and when I don't seem convinced she adds, "I could never become an alcoholic. I feel sick too quickly and I hate the feeling the following morning." After giving me a brief embrace, she pushes me aside, gets into her car and drives off deliberately slowly.

On my way home the meadows are steaming in the summer heat, fireflies hover in the Rosental woods, and for a few seconds I'm in a state of total contentment.

On the day after the concert I feel uneasy in the quiet of my flat. For a long time I was calmed by not feeling the presence of anybody around me, but now I suddenly find it oppressive. I escape to the lake, then the allotment, and I don't come home until the evening.

When a message arrives on my phone I flinch.

Dear Linda, I saw you on the meadow yesterday, but unfortunately only when the heavens opened. Thanks for your letter and don't worry – I can take it! I'd really like to see you. Just let me know when you're ready. Love, Esther.

Her wedding is in a fortnight. In my letter I said that I didn't have the strength for such a gathering, but that I was happy for her and would like to meet up another time. I read her message again, especially that particular phrase. It was something she often said and each time I got goose pimples. *I can take it*, she'd say, meaning my indescribable pain. Sometimes these words lurked in my mind for hours. *I can take it*. They repelled me, and the more frequently she uttered them, the more I heard something else in the phrase. I wouldn't have been more shocked if she'd said *Your blood's tasty*. Of course you can take it, I thought, you're not the one suffering here! It's not your child who's died. Not your life that's been destroyed. I believed that Esther was clinging to my soul, feeding off me like a parasite. Nobody does anything good without getting something for it, Richard said, even if it was a feeling of superiority. He called her an *strength-sapper*. And he was right. Now my body remembers the old distrust and can't think about supper anymore. It will only allow me a weak tea before I go to bed, without having answered Esther.

13

A few days later the flickering flame of my life propels me to the east of the city. I allow myself to be steered to a bleak, treeless street, at the end of which is a flat-roofed industrial building. Via some outside steps I come to a metal door leading to a long corridor. Behind the second door on the left I can hear Rammstein and I know I'm in the right place. I enter quietly. Richard is standing with his back to me. Arms crossed and head slightly cocked, he's gazing at the empty canvas on the easel in front of him.

Still unnoticed I allow my gaze to roam through the room. Leaning against the wall to the right are new large paintings; by the wall to the left, boxes are piled metres high.

I don't want to have to call his name; I'd rather he turn around, see me and feel happy. I think this *at him* with all the power of my mind and he turns and smiles.

After a long embrace he gives me a tour and shows me the mezzanine, accessed via metal stairs without a banister, and where he has a bed, a clothes rack on wheels and a chest of drawers. Downstairs in the windowless bathroom all I see is Richard's toothbrush, his shaving cream and the shampoo he's been using for twenty years. The small galley kitchen with a two-flame gas cooker has everything you need to cook and there are dirty dishes in the sink.

He runs a hand through his hair and a resigned smile appears on his face. "Brida's daughters are both there, working through some stuff that happened in their childhood . . . their *traumas*." He looks dismissive.

"I see. What about the two of you?"

He sighs and takes his time to answer.

"The truth is, Brida isn't interested in having a partner, just a dependable lover. She's too busy with her own life. But you know I'm a family man – being together day in, day out isn't a punishment."

I'm amused by his choice of words.

"Fancy a coffee?" he says.

While he fills the moka pot, I take a look at the canvas.

"It's a cycle of five paintings," he calls over to me.

Three are finished and two more are to come. At first glance these are everyday scenes – a slightly overweight woman in skinny jeans and a tight top outside a shopping centre, a girl sticking out her tongue as she takes a selfie in front of the Bach statue – but on closer inspection you can see gossamer-thin threads on the arms and legs. These are marionettes, operated by an invisible puppeteer.

The third painting is the most impressive: a person with a muscular torso, large breasts, almond eyes, brown skin and long hair. They have a neatly trimmed beard and they're wearing a sequinned dress with spaghetti straps. Attached to their upper arm is a device to measure bodily functions and they have AirPods in their ears. Sitting crookedly beside them, and with its tongue hanging out, is a French bulldog, the product of what's known as "torture breeding" because the animal, its anatomy bred for purely aesthetic reasons, suffers from serious health problems.

All three paintings have a pull, the like of which I've never seen in Richard's work before. I can't take my eyes off the picture of the person in the sequinned dress with the dog. There's something absurd and artificial about the figure, which fascinates and repels me in equal measure.

"Through Brida I've met a gallerist." Richard hands me a cup of coffee. "He's seriously interested."

"That's great. What's his name?"

"You probably won't know him. His gallery's in Hamburg."

And indeed I haven't heard the name. He only deals in painting and sculpture, Richard says, reeling off a few names. I know one of the artists – a sculptor.

"The fluid, fully digitally networked individual, who is voluntarily under surveillance," Richard says, having noticed me staring at the painting. "That's the future. Or at least one possible variant – even a utopia for some."

"I think the way you let it stand, without passing judgment, is so good. A really strong perspective. And it's beautifully painted. You've refined your technique."

"I've been spending a lot of time in the studio."

He shows me sketches for another picture in the cycle. A line of electricity pylons and mobile phone masts in a huge maize field; in the foreground a girl in a hoodie, drawing at an easel.

"Your talented pupil?" I ask.

He nods. "She's fantastic. Completely independent. A free spirit."

He closes his eyes for a moment.

"Are you alright?"

"Exhausted," he says, reaching for a folding chair which he puts in the middle of the room. From there he surveys the paintings. "Perhaps they need titles. What do you think?"

"Might enhance the impact, but I'm not sure they're absolutely necessary."

From the way he's sitting there, slightly crumpled, it seems as if he's put all his energy into these pictures without leaving anything for himself. His cheeks are sunken and the hard lines make his face even more striking.

"Have you lost weight?" I ask.

"Yes, a bit."

He looks distinctly uncomfortable as he heaves himself out of the chair and says, "Maybe I'm just getting old."

He wanders over to some pictures leaning against the wall and sets them out in a row on the floor. "He wants to show my series of portraits too."

In the middle I can see Esther's profile with the beautiful back of her head.

"Your friend," Richard says.

She's not my friend, I almost reply. More positively I say, "I'm seeing her tomorrow. For the first time in ages."

He looks at me but doesn't enquire further. Instead he turns to the paintings.

At the door he sweeps a strand of hair behind my ear before giving me a gentle peck on the cheek. As I'm making my way out of the building the heavy bass of Rammstein is already hammering against the wall of his studio.

The following day I'm greeted by a warm, cloudy and wind-still morning. Outside I bump into the wife of the paediatric surgeon who's heading swiftly for the Rosental, her boy holding her hand and the baby in the sling. The antipathy is mutual and I take a detour to avoid having to exchange pleasantries. When I arrive at our meeting point – the peace oak in the Rosental – I see her with another woman and two children at the window that gives a view of the giraffes in the zoo.

Esther beams at me. Her hair is long and her updo emphasises the beautiful back of her head. As she takes my arm she whispers that I can have no idea how pleased she is to see me, and that I needn't worry about what I wrote in my letter – *she can take it.*

My legs almost give way. Still trapped in her firm embrace, less than ten seconds after having said hello, I know that our friendship isn't going to be revived. As if numbed I stroll with her around the great meadow and the pond, and ask her questions only so I don't have to talk about myself. I hear about the trips she's been on with her husband and those they're intending to do. He's from a very modest background, she tells me, and has worked his way right up, so sometimes he needs to show off a bit. She laughs. In autumn, as soon as the days get shorter and the weather deteriorates, they're off to Dubai where they'll stay in a luxury hotel with all the frills: a delayed honeymoon. If I'd made a suggestion like that to Richard, he'd have merely raised his left eyebrow. As if she's able to read my thoughts Esther pauses, stops and looks at me. Her face is remarkably smooth and firm.

"How do you manage to look so fresh?" I ask. I'm genuinely interested.

She hesitates for a moment and gives a coy smile. "Vampire lift. Platelet-rich plasma. Produced from my own blood and injected below the skin. Completely normal in the film world. I don't know of a single actress over forty who hasn't had any work. They all have something done. Botox, thread lifts, eyelid surgery. But a vampire lift looks most natural."

I'm almost certain that I *would have had some work done* too, in a different life, a life in which it makes a difference whether your skin is radiant or saggy. I move on from this topic to ask about Esther's job as I keep walking at a brisk pace. She must notice my discomfort. Together with her here I don't like myself, and when we're back at the peace oak, having done the round, I stop.

"I'm sorry, Esther, but I can't."

Her cheeks are red and her lips are quivering slightly – a perfect doll's face, compared to which mine must look like that of an old woman.

"We've got nothing in common. It's as if I'm living in a different world."

I can't bring myself to spell out more truths; I can immediately see the shock in her face.

"Let's bring this to a friendly conclusion, Esther," I beg her.

She's battling tears but spares me further questions. "Yes, I understand."

Beneath the canopy of the oak that's more than one hundred and fifty years old we hug one last time.

"Thanks for the good times," I whisper, then walk away.

I don't turn around. With every step I take away from Esther my relief grows that I didn't extricate myself from this without saying anything. Only now do I realise how heavily everything unsaid and unresolved has been weighing down on me. I return to my quiet, tidy flat in the hope that she might be feeling something similar. A burden has been lifted from me. Yet I feel sad. My former self would have sought a distraction, a reward – a new dress, lipstick. But here in my third life I sit on a chair in my kitchen and allow all the emotions to flow.

14

In August I get a message from Klaus. *Your godchild has arrived!!!*, he writes, adding three laughing emojis. A few minutes later there's a photo of Bruni and an alpaca with white fur and brown patches behind the ears. Both are beaming, the alpaca almost from ear to ear, and I wonder whether this grin is a breeding goal. At any rate, sheer happiness shines in Bruni's eyes. This lucky charm's name is Molly, Klaus writes, and he asks when I can come to meet her.

This week! I reply, replying to the photo of Bruni and Molly with three heart-eyes emojis.

That same day I notice that Brida and Richard's allotment is starting to show signs of neglect. After the cold snap in spring the plants they put in recently have really shot up, the lawn has luxuriant growth and the vegetables in the raised beds are thriving, but the weeds, whose seeds were scattered to every corner of the plot when it was turned over, are racing ahead and it looks as if they haven't been tackled for weeks. The most successful plant is the thorn apple and the two gardeners don't appear to be doing anything to stop it spreading. They were on holiday in the south of England, but must be back by now.

In those rare hours when Natascha and I are busy in the garden together, Nina is often here too, swinging in her hanging chair on the small terrace and composing crazy melodies from her inexhaustible repertoire. A Mozart sonata segues into a children's song, which then forms the beginning of a Bach partita, which in turn leads into a Christmas carol and so on. Occasionally we stop what we're doing, look at each other, smile, shake our heads, then thrust our hands into the earth again. But the autumn is looming and with it the end of growth in the garden, as well as the structure it imposes on me. I need another meaningful task.

At the end of the month I sign on with a volunteering agency. They're looking for substitute grandparents, people to visit the elderly and homework supervisors. Anything to do with children is out of the question for me, so, from September onwards, I pay one or two visits a week to Frau Engel, an eighty-three-year-old widow who lives in a two-room flat in a concrete block to the west of the centre. We take an instant liking to each other. If the weather's nice we'll go for a walk in the nearby park where I read her articles from the *Leipziger Volkszeitung*. She prefers the benches close to the duck pond or by Luther Church. As soon as I start reading she says, "Louder!" Frau Engel stubbornly refuses to use her hearing aid; after a few cautious attempts to persuade her to do so I give up.

If it's rainy or windy we stay in her flat where I read to her too, mostly contemporary fiction borrowed from the city library. In future I'm also going to go with her to concerts at the Gewandhaus, where she has an annual subscription. She's paying, of course.

Frau Engel is tiny, with thin, mahogany-coloured hair that she keeps tied back with a ruby-red, velvet-covered clasp. Her skin is like tissue paper. She likes to wear bold colours and she tells me she needs two hours for her morning toilette. "The older you get the more time you need to sort yourself out, so you don't get a terrible shock when you look in the mirror."

She used to be a professor of linguistics, she doesn't have any children and when she hears my story she tells me I'm wasting my time with her; I ought to be looking for a proper job instead. I ought to be thinking of my retirement, she says. You need money when you're older! There's nothing worse than having to live in poverty through the last decades of your life, which are difficult enough as it is. She works out what she needs each month to be able to play at least some part in the city's social life, to be able to afford cultural events, the hairdresser and pedicures, decent food and the Japanese premium sencha tea that she drinks every morning. The last pension information I got is nowhere near the figure she comes up with. Frau Engel scares me, and she says that was precisely her intention.

Because of her I start looking for jobs but my search within a radius of one hundred kilometres doesn't locate a single opportunity for an art curator. I could apply in Bonn, Duisburg or Munich, and in Karlsruhe there's an interesting ad for a job focusing on fine art and performance, but I'm not going to leave this city. Sonja's grave is here, as are the few people who are important to me.

Something needs to happen; Frau Engel has shown me that. In her life I see my future – alone, in a one-bedroom flat with a volunteer visitor who pops in from time to time.

The surprising thing about this is that I can envisage a future at all.

Then, on one morning that still has some summer warmth, Richard calls and asks if we can meet. He speaks slowly, drawing out his words, as if each one were draining him of energy. I ask whether everything's alright and he answers with a flippant "Yeah, yeah".

The following day we meet at the Italian restaurant around the corner. He seems even more haggard than last time, his walking is slow and stooped, and there's an odd look of astonishment on his face. Before we take our places at a table by the window I ask him what's wrong. He shakes his head, sits down, skims the menu and hands it to me. He doesn't want anything apart from water. When we've ordered he takes a deep breath and begins to talk. When he tells me of the stomach cramps he's had for years and which are getting worse, his frequent bowel movements – sometimes bloody and uncontrolled – weight loss and chronic exhaustion, I think I know what's coming. He's already had blood tests, a colonoscopy and an MRI, all of which he went through on his own. During the week of tests Brida was on a reading tour in Austria and Switzerland.

Voices, lights, movements fade into the distance. Richard stares at the tabletop.

"Bowel cancer," I say.

He looks up, shaking his head.

"Colitis ulcerosa, an inflammation of the digestive system. It started after Sonja's death. I didn't take it seriously, ignored it for too long. At the moment I'm on medication but the inflammation isn't getting any better, it's too far advanced. Now there's a danger that the corroded intestines will tear. I should've started treatment much earlier. Since the last flare-up there are some days when I have to go to the loo thirty times. How can I teach with that? I'm on sick leave, I mean, I always have to be near a loo. There's no quality of life anymore, it's just . . ."

He shakes his head and turns away, and I feel on the verge

of displacement behaviour, a dreadful case of the giggles that I can barely keep a lid on. My right leg begins twitching uncontrollably.

Richard continues talking in a flat voice. "The doctors have advised me to have surgery. The entire colon and rectum have to go. I'll keep my sphincter and somehow they'll cobble together a connection between the small intestine and the anal canal. But maybe it'll come down to a stoma. You can even go swimming with one of those, did you know that?"

No, I didn't.

"I've got my first major solo exhibition in December. Strange, isn't it? Right now . . ."

Not wanting to interrupt him I say nothing.

"I know there's no point in looking for reasons, but . . ." His voice cracks, he clears his throat and continues, "But if everything goes smoothly I'll be halfway fit again in a few months. That's a possibility. Given my lifestyle, seeing as I don't drink or smoke, it's not so improbable.

My food comes; I leave it untouched. Richard speaks of his fear, but also of a total change in his perception, of viewing life from the endpoint. And he says he doesn't love Brida. He desires her but he doesn't love her. He assumes it's mutual. The situation is all too much for her.

"I don't want her to accompany me on this path."

He looks at me, holding my gaze for a long while.

"I've no idea how things are going to go from here, Linda. But I'd really like to see more of you in the next few months."

I shift my chair closer to his and lay my hands on his face.

"You don't have to get through this alone. I'm here. I'll be with you."

His head sinks heavily in my hands and then he places his hands on mine. We sit like this for a while. The waitresses give our table a wide berth and pack up my food so I can take it with me. When we leave they're effusive with their kind words and good wishes.

That evening I listen to music with Frau Engel. Her top-quality speakers send the purest sound into every corner of her sitting room. I point out that the neighbours might complain. "The neighbours are hard of hearing too," Frau Engel exclaims cheerfully. "Only the elderly live here."

But then she picks up the remote control and it is silent.

"What's wrong?" she asks. "You look like you've seen a ghost."

Without hesitation I tell her about Richard. She waits for a moment, then says, "Every family has their sorrows. And these sorrows demand Schubert's Piano trio No.2 in E flat. You can have a good weep to that. Especially the *Andante con moto*."

We sit beside each other on the sofa, Frau Engel smooths down her skirt and closes her eyes when the first note plays. We listen to the *Allegro*, then the *Andante con moto* and I cry as if on cue. Frau Engel switches off the music afterwards.

"I want you to promise me something," she says. "I've come across too many intelligent women who've sacrificed themselves. First they look after the children, then they care for their parents and finally their husband. After all that they're exhausted and they die. Support your husband but find the right balance, Linda. And work again."

"I promise I'll find another job. But as far as my husband's concerned, it's not a sacrifice, it's decency."

"But the boundary between decency and sacrifice is fluid," she says calmly. "And you're still a young woman."

I laugh out loud; Frau Engel gives me a stern look.

"You're forty years younger than me, Linda! *Forty*! If I'd

known how young I was when I was your age." She smiles and sighs. "But I had no idea."

These words go through my head half the night. Despite the tablets I wake up hourly. I resist the urge to swallow another pill and also defy the temptation to reach for my phone, deactivate flight mode and send a message to Richard. Tomorrow I wouldn't remember what I'd written or that I had written at all.

I get up long before sunrise, switch on the phone and message Natascha. We meet at hers for breakfast. Nina, who's been going to a support group for a few weeks, has already been picked up by a driver. Natascha is still in her nightie. Her thick plait hangs over her shoulder and when she puts the coffee on she tosses it behind her. She listens as I talk about Richard and Frau Engel, sets the table quietly, puts frozen rolls in the oven, cuts an avocado in half and stirs three eggs into a pan with hot olive oil. Handing me my coffee she says impassively, "Another example of how pointless it is to make plans."

But then we remember that we too once viewed life differently, set ourselves targets and conceived of our future happiness. As young women we imagined how as elderly women we'd look after our grandchildren within a large family. We too had fallen under the spell of these potent images – ghastly but beautiful – and when they, like a dying star, fell into the eternal darkness, we fell with them. Are we smarter now?

"Definitely smarter," Natascha says. "But the stupid heart hopes for a miracle nonetheless."

"Always this *nonetheless*," I say. "It's what drives us on."

Nodding, Natascha holds up a clenched fist and repeats it. "Nonetheless."

I also clench my fist and say it out loud. "Nonetheless!"

Then we laugh, I look at Natascha and am glad to have her as a friend.

15

We enter the hospital and leave normality. On this gorgeous day, with a bright-blue sky and a low but still powerful autumn sun, we dive into the world of symptoms, diagnoses, treatment plans and medical prescriptions. Everyday things lose their significance. Shopping lists, work on the allotment, the weather, the book I'm reading, the appointments I've made, the repair of the dripping tap in the bathroom, putting on the winter tyres.

We wait. Together with other people who are either quietly anxious or cursing with impatience, Richard fills out a questionnaire while I stare at signs showing the emergency escape plan and an art print in loud colours. When his name is called I'm hoping it's going to be a doctor who looks Richard in the eye before they begin talking. One who offers their hand in greeting and listens first, rather than gazing at the puzzling black-and-white MRT or CT images. In other words, someone with human understanding.

Richard knows the score; he's been through a lot already. He'll be admitted today and operated on tomorrow. While we wait, I learn from listening to the other people chatting that the doctors work through their normal daily schedule and only fit in the new arrivals when they can. That's why the whole procedure sometimes drags long into the afternoon. Now hungry, I rummage in my bag. On the advice of a nurse we've brought along some food: apples, bananas, nuts and dried fruit for me; a Thermos of vegetable broth and a bottle of water for Richard. He takes small sips of the hot soup, leans his head towards me and says quietly, "It's strange. Apparently our generation has such a high life expectancy."

Then everything goes quicker than expected. In a tiny consultation room they take Richard's blood pressure, do an ECG, take blood and make a note of his height and weight. The anaesthetist explains the risks of the anaesthetic, asks about dentures or wobbly teeth because of the intubation and notifies the surgeon. At the door he turns around, smiles and says, "Do you know the difference between a surgeon and God? – God knows he's not a surgeon."

More than anything it's the look of horror on the nurse's face that makes us burst out laughing after a brief moment of shock, and when the surgeon comes sweeping into the room soon afterwards, she giggles too. "Did my colleague crack another of his jokes?" the surgeon says, shaking his head. "I hope it was a good one."

He introduces himself, sits down, opens the file and describes the procedure. Then he pauses to allow the information to sink in, before pointing out that this kind of operation is one of the most demanding in abdominal surgery, outlining the recovery in the best- and worst-case scenarios, and explaining the overall prognosis. Which is good, in his opinion. There's reason to be confident.

"Be brave!" he says before leaving the room as energetically as he entered it.

We go to the ward reception, where an orderly with warrior-like tattoos and a confusingly high-pitched voice explains tomorrow's schedule. At eight o'clock Richard will report nil-by-mouth to the ward, move into his room and get a wristband with his name. He'll put his clothes in the wardrobe, lock it and give the key to a nurse or an orderly, put on the hospital gown, lie down in bed, have a cannula inserted into the vein and wait until they come to take him, with the bed, into the basement where the operating theatres are. He'll be met by an orderly and passed to the anaesthetist. If he wants he could have something to calm him prior to the actual anaesthetic. But Richard doesn't want anything.

"I'm not scared," he says and I know he's lying. His eyes are as wide as saucers.

"Everything clear so far?" the orderly asks.

Richard nods politely.

Then he's allowed to go home, and today his home is at mine. It's only late morning and neither of us wants to spend the rest of the day in the flat. In the dazzling light of a blazing sun, the sole ruler of the sky, we drive to Lake Cospuden and wander to a quiet bathing spot amongst young trees. The night-time temperature has been in single figures for a while now and I reckon the lake is between ten and twelve degrees. We spread out a blanket, eat what we've brought with us, gaze across the water, on the surface of which floats a carpet of colourful leaves, and reflect on the days when the two of us were healthy without having to question the fact, and took the soundness of our bodies for granted. I lean my head on his shoulder and we talk about how incredibly happy we were when Sonja was alive and we were a family. Ducks swim past close to the shore and further out a pair of swans. Richard gets up and starts taking his clothes off.

"In the end," he says, before going into the water, "all you can do is hope for God's mercy."

A jolt shoots through my body. These are alien words from his lips. I quickly take my clothes off too and then we swim in the cold water until it's painful and we begin to shiver.

Back home Richard is still freezing. While he's having a hot shower I sit on the balcony with a glass of wine and gaze at the wall of ivy where the sparrows are making a racket. Through the open balcony door I hear his phone ringing. It stops then starts again. A third attempt goes unanswered too.

Late that afternoon we sit by candlelight in the kitchen. I eat tinned sardines, bread and carrots, while Richard drinks an entire litre of laxative and two litres of tea over the course of several hours. He spends the evening on the loo, and not for the first time either. He's set up his laptop on a chair and he's watching *The Big Lebowski*. Occasionally I hear him laugh. When I've made his bed on the pull-out sofa and turn in myself he's still sitting there.

In the morning, during the fifteen-minute drive to the hospital, he phones Brida. It doesn't appear to bother him that I can hear every word.

"I didn't 'just leave'," he says gently. "I explained it to you. Our relationship is nowhere near that stage where you endure everything together and put up with your partner no matter what state they're in." For a while he listens as he peers out of the window and drums his fingers on his thigh. "You didn't do anything wrong, Brida. If it were the other way around I wouldn't know how to cope with it either. And of course you can visit me. It's just that today I need someone by my side who I don't have to explain anything to, someone I trust implicitly. Linda's here with me, we're already on our way to hospital. She'll call you after the operation, OK?"

He looks at me, his eyebrows raised, and I nod.

The list of people I've got to call includes Richard's parents, who've said they'll visit tomorrow; Ylvie, who really wants to come but is expecting her fifth child anytime in the next few days; Arvid, who's been living in Naples for a year since finishing his Masters; Hauke and Brida. I stop at the taxi parking spot right outside the hospital and instinctively reach for Richard's hands. They're dry and cold; I rub them warm and say, "It's going to be fine. This isn't the end."

He smiles.

"One time you came to visit me in the village you wanted the two of us to go on a trip," I remind him. "To find out what was left of us."

"Yes, but you didn't want to."

"I couldn't."

"I know." The friendly look on his face makes it easy for me to keep speaking.

"As soon as you're better . . ." I say.

Richard nods with the hint of a smile. "OK," he says solemnly. "Let's do it." Then he lays his hands, now warm, on my face, gives me a goodbye kiss and gets out.

I watch him go, his bag over his shoulder, up the steps to the entrance. At the top he turns, waves and blows me a kiss. I return the gesture.

The nurses on the ward will contact me as soon as he wakes up. He's got his living will on him, a second copy of which is in my bag. For now all I can do is wait.

The day is still young. On the back seat are a Thermos of tea and a large towel. As I'm about to drive off, I see in the wing mirror a young girl with a high ponytail arriving on a racer. She gets off, secures her bike and skips up the steps to the hospital. My heart misses a beat.

I sit there in silence for a few minutes. I inhale and exhale. Then I drive out of the city to the lake.

Acknowledgements

First of all I would like to thank, as ever, my publisher Philipp Keel and all the staff at Diogenes Verlag, especially Susanne von Ledebur and my editor Kati Hertzsch. Once the lonely work on the manuscript is finished, the collaborative project begins. The enthusiasm and care all of those involved, and who I'm so reliant on, was palpable, and it made the work a pleasure.

Thanks are also due to everyone who helped me find the time to write. In the first instance these include the friends and helpers of my younger daughter, especially Lena Wingerter, Lene Stange, Vanessa Holze and Mandy Reinschk.

Huge thanks to Judy Lybke and Peter Hartwig for providing me with a wonderful refuge. There I was able to solve the problems that almost prevented this text from coming to fruition.

I'd also like to thank all my friends and acquaintances who open up and tell me their stories. There isn't the space to list them all here. Some are given a voice in the book; from others I've borrowed an idea, a phrase or a particularly lovely or apposite word.

Finally, thanks to Steffen, Clara and Rosa. Without them and their love, everything else would be meaningless.

DANIELA KRIEN is the author of four novels and a collection of short stories. *Someday We'll Tell Each Other Everything* (2013) was adapted for film by Emily Atef, and *Love in Five Acts* (2021) and *The Fire* (2023) were bestsellers in Germany and translated into many languages. She has two daughters and lives in Leipzig.

JAMIE BULLOCH is the translator of more than fifty books from German, and has twice won the Schlegel-Tieck Prize. The authors he has translated include Robert Menasse, Birgit Vanderbeke, Timur Vermes, Arno Geiger, David Safier and Sebastian Fitzek.